SO-AFH-951

SKEWED

FLASH FICTION

A Collection of 50 Freaky-Fast Reads

by Mary B. Good

© 2017 Mary B. Good

ISBN: 978-1-935920-62-5

All rights reserved.
This book, or parts thereof, may not be reproduced in any form without permission from the author; exceptions are made for brief excerpts used in reviews.

Printed in the USA
2nd Edition

Publisher's Express Press
www.PublishersExpressPress.com

To Mimi

Thanks to: My manuscript doctor, Michele Gerard Good; Genie Campbell Rostad, technical editor; Toni Woodruff Eckmayer, Kindle proofreader; Sandy Dantzman, book production; Larry Johns, publishers rep; Mike Elling, publisher and all those that helped in one way or another, Mary Nellis, Gloria Welniak, Sharon Huettle, Sandy Bredesen, Tom Ziegler, Kristofer Simmons, Marcia MacMurray, Jim Hoffman, Nancy Carroll, Evan Wing, Mary Palumbo, Grant Gillespie, Dee Dee Berek, Ania Stawarz De Lorey, Angel and all the rest. You know who you are!

Mary B. Good

PREFACE

Have you got time for an offbeat ala skewed tale, an amusing experience, something thought-provoking, maybe something that bites? These are people stories: party people, funny people, lazy people, frightened people, quirky people, greedy people, curious people and others. These stories are about beloved imaginary friends in the altered reality of my mind.   MBG

Disclaimer: All similarity to persons living or dead is purely coincidental. If you see yourself in a story, it's not you!

I know you don't have time for the likes of *War and Peace*, my dear reader, and with my flash fiction you don't need to. You can read one of my short stories in less time than it takes to hang up on a robo caller. Half the stories are but one-minute reads. All are less than four minutes for the average reader.

For your convenience, word count and approximate reading time is at the top of each short story, so you don't have to waste your Facebook time reading something that drones on for three minutes when you only have two. But don't hold me to it; some people read faster than others, some slower. Also included is a moral or quizlet at the end of each story, but don't look for wise counsel, because these aren't necessarily relevant to the story. TITLES in the content are uniquely marked in different type faces as noted below, according to their approximate reading times:

STORIES THREE MINUTES MORE OR LESS

Stories Two Minutes More Or Less

Stories One Minute More Or Less

CONTENTS

INTRODUCTION

Flash fiction is a short story wearing a girdle. We squeeze in and climb out! Flash fiction can't stand lengthy introductions. We just get on with it. Read it and enjoy! If you're not hooked by the third paragraph, don't linger, move on to the next story. Enough said.

MBG

The Fantasy Party

Word Count: 660
Reading Time: just under two minutes 45 seconds

Big Bertha was a very heavy woman confined to a wheelchair. She was simply too heavy for her legs to hold her up. She was bigger than life, but Bertha's imagination was bigger than life too.

She loved food, fun and because she was housebound flights of fancy. One nagging, recurring daydream involved being surrounded by drop-dead handsome men doting on her, feeding her kissing her.

Playful Bertha entertained thoughts of a fantasy party that never could be, but always would be, in her mind. The big one conjured up an all-male guest list with every old boyfriend she ever had, and every man she ever admired from afar. At Bertha's party, if any guy on the guest list dared to bring a date, the unwanted girlfriend or wife would be shown the door, post haste. Only male servers comprised the wait staff. Bertha, and Bertha alone, commanded 100% of all the men's attention.

Omar Sharif as he appeared in *Lawrence of Arabia* and Robert Redford took turns feeding her caviar from an itty bitty spoon as she lounged on a fainting couch. Cary Grant sipped Dom Perignon with her. Liam Neeson put chocolate-covered strawberries on her tongue.

She was serenaded by Robert Goulet who sang, *If Ever I Would Leave You*, and Keanu Reeves gave her love notes he pulled out of the mailbox in *The Lake House.*

George Clooney told her clever jokes, Humphrey Bogart blew smoke in her face and whispered, "we'll always have Paris," just as he did in *Casablanca*; Christopher Reeve did a trick for her, where he kept morphing back and forth somewhere in time.

It delighted the lady with the still-pretty face, when Johnny Depp came to her fantasy party as Tonto, in full war paint with a dead bird on his head.

Near the end of the party, for an over-the-top finale, the late, great Patrick Swayze, invited as Bertha's guest-of-honor/dance partner, strolled in, removed his black leather jacket and headed straight for her saying, "Nobody puts Big Bertha in the corner." With that, he extended his hand to her, lifted the big one gracefully from her chair and gently led her to the dance floor, where all the men's eyes were glued on her.

Patrick and Bertha started artfully *"Dirty Dancing,"* with Patrick pulling off the awesome lift like he did in that film, only this time, instead of 'Baby,' Big Bertha made the running, herculean leap into his outstretched arms and was horizontally balanced high in the air. Effortlessly. Picture it: three hundred pounds 'wortha' Bertha suspended two and half feet over Swayze's head, supported, maybe, with one arm. Heaven!

Bertha fantasized so much about her party she believed it was real. When she told her sister, Ariacne, that she had a party the other night, and she danced with Patrick Swayze, Bertha's sister was skeptical.

The next morning Ariacne dropped in to see her, and Bertha told her about how Johnny Depp was there, wearing war paint with a dead bird on his head, and even gave her the dead bird as a love token.

"He did," insisted Bertha, "he really did. "And he kissed me too. He got paint all over my face."

She was hysterical when Ariacne rolled her eyes.

It's true. It's true. Believe me," hollered Bertha.

"OK, then, where's the dead bird?" Ariacne asked.

"I buried it!" replied Bertha, "But I had it, I did."

"To change the subject," said Ariacne, slowly and in a low voice, "Good news, honey. I've got a date for you."

In the last decade, Bertha had been keeping company exclusively with Jack Daniels, so the prospect of a date with a real flesh-and-blood man made her ecstatic.

"Who is he? What's his name? What does he do? Is he a lawyer, an accountant, an actor?" Bertha asked.

"No," said her sister, "I got you a date with a shrink."

Quizlet: Does it really matter if Keanu Reeves can act?

The Genius

Word Count: 398
Reading Time: just over a minute 30 seconds

Humphrey Dumphrey had a plump body and a pin head with a brain the size of a chicken's. He was so round, you could almost roll him down the street. But Humphrey exercised that teeny-tiny brain to capacity, unlike normal people who use very little of their brain power. The man was, in fact, a genius.

From youth, Hump was no dumb cluck; he had a mission to save the world. He became a doctor, a medical researcher and a lab rat. His whole life was the laboratory, 24/7. Humphrey had no friends, no wife, no social life, no time to rest.

Dr. Dumphrey used his time for noble purposes. He came "this close" to finding a cure for the common cold and was "almost there" on his quest to cure cancer. The good doctor was working simultaneously on his theory to end all mental disease by rebooting the brain, much like one would reboot a computer.

His idea was radical, on the cutting edge, so to speak, and experiments were successful on rats and monkeys during umpteen medical trials but had never been attempted on human beings. Lacking a volunteer subject, Dr. Dumphrey decided to undergo the bizarre procedure: decapitation and reconstructive surgery.

After years of meticulous research, planning and extensive preparation by an 18-man medical team, Hump was on the operating table. Doctors worked for hours on this special patient.

Surgeons started severing the skull at the brain stem level and realized that the medical instruments they were using weren't sharp enough to slice through the cranium. The medical team was dumbfounded with the bizarre finding that Humphrey's noggin was harder than quartz. The Good Lord had created Humphrey with a nearly-impenetrable skull to cradle his precious, sui generis brain.

Staff rushed to find an industrial-strength power tool to do the job. This delayed the surgery; by the time they tried to reattach his head to his body hours later, the complications were insurmountable. They couldn't put Humphrey Dumphrey back together again.

Doctors called it a day, and the custodian turned off the lights in the surgical suite.

The fingers on the corpse's right hand moved to form the thumbs up sign. Humphrey's head, perched in the toxic waste disposal bin, struggled to send this message from his brain: "Don't give up! Not yet!"

Moral of the story: Humphrey was "this close" to staying alive.

Real Or Fake

Word Count: 303
Reading Time: a minute 15 seconds

Sister Amy was a Roman Catholic nun and art expert often called to art museums across the country. Sister authenticated works presumably painted by Manet, Monet Dali and others. Amy could spot a fake from the across the room, she was that good at what she did.

The work brought the nuns needed income, and Sister Amy did quite well, so she branched out as a certified document examiner. She became a major player in the business.

Sotheby's came calling one transformative day. They had reservations about the validity and value of a three-word document the owner hoped to put on the auction block for a million dollars.

The letter was written on parchment of a quality never seen before, the source of ink on the paper was unknown and the unusual handwriting was unlike any other. Sister Amy spent a fruitless two weeks researching the document.

The owner of the auction item made the ridiculous assertion that it came to him one Saturday as the first and only written communication from outer space. He further claimed that the letter-writer was an alien being. The words on the single page read only, "Are you listening?"

Sister Amy was determined to get to the bottom of this bizarre assignment.

The story of the nun researching an intriguing million-dollar mystery went viral. The media jumped on it. Now the whole world waited impatiently for the defining pronouncement of Sister Amy, leading authority and examiner extraordinaire!

Ten million viewers were glued to their TV sets as David Muir introduced Sister Amy during a network news spot.

"No one's going to believe this, David," she said.

And they didn't.

Her professional credibility was destroyed when Sister Amy announced to the world the message was from God.

Quizlet: Just wondering—Does UPS deliver on the Sabbath?

The Entertainers

Word Count: 528
Reading Time: just over two minutes

Dolores Montalban and Ricardo del Rio were childhood sweethearts whose families lived on the same block in Barcelona. Both sets of parents immigrated to Mexico around the time of Pancho Villa and the Mexican Revolution.

The two married, and like many others in search of a better life, the couple crossed the border and waded the Rio Grande into Texas. They came as immigrants and stayed as braceros. The couple made their way to Escondido where they heard there were fruit farms.

Dolores and Ricardo tired after a year of picking strawberries and longed for a glamorous life. They moved to Hollywood and became entertainers. Dolores, especially, had illusions of grandeur and wanted to see her name up in lights.

It was rough at first; eventually Ricardo found work as a stunt man. He enjoyed the thrill of stunt doubling for Antonio Banderas and Javiar Bardem, although he never personally met them. His best stunt was falling off a cliff in a Benicio del Torro film which unfortunately wound up on the cutting floor. But it was a living, and give or take a broken collar bone here or fractured femur there, he was satisfied with his lot.

Dolores continued to seek work as an actress. She assumed the stage name Chickie Boom Boom and soon got a part in a soft porn movie. But when the bedroom scene was scheduled to shoot, her pangs of conscience and strict Catholic upbringing made Chickie chicken out.

She left smut with a moral victory and a chance to go into horror. She dropped the Chickie and changed her stage name to Cloris Blucher, a move that got her a walk-on part in a little-known Roger Corman thriller, *Attack of the Pickle Puss People*. She was one of a band of gherkins.

Most of the time, Dolores suffered the ravages of the casting department: "You're too tall, too short, too old, too young, too fat, too thin, too dark, too blonde or not blonde enough." What really hurt was, "You're not Hispanic enough," even when she changed her name to Lupe.

After paying her dues on a series of poorly made B-flops, Dolores/Chickie/Cloris/Lupe got the big break that would propel her to stardom and a place on the Hollywood Walk of Fame. Here was her chance to work in a Steven Spielberg film tentatively titled, *The Day They Put Old Dixie Down*, the story of a wounded war horse during the War of 1812. She had a supporting part as the nurse who puts on the horse's feedbag.

Looking forward to seeing one of her names at the bottom of the credits, she was on top of the world. But her dream of stardom soon faded; the production hit a snag. After a major rewrite, *Down* was dropped due to lack of financing. And it turned out Spielberg wasn't even involved, just speculation. After years of frustration and disappointment, the failed actress was beaten. Hollywood chewed her up and spit her out. You can find her in the Valley, working as the night manager at Burger King.

Moral of the story: If you aspire to be a Hollywood star, don't!

Destiny

Word Count: 306 words
Reading Time: a minute 15 seconds

Dolores Lamas, aka Chickie Boom Boom, aka Cloris Bucher aka Lupe, the failed actress, became bitter after a long period of watching others make it in Hollywood.

Then one day, she got a knock on the door. It was Publisher's Clearing House. All those entries had paid off. Dolores had won five million dollars!

Suddenly, all her lost Hollywood hopes of what could have been, now became her "will be again." Dolores dusted off her dreams and told her husband, Ricardo, he need never risk his life again doing stunts for movies that often put him in the hospital.

The thrilled winner immediately called Burger King and quit her job.

Dolores announced that she would use the big bucks to buy a Hollywood studio and call it Dolric Pictures. Ricardo would be the head honcho, and she would star in movies they produced.

"I'll do lunch with Tom Hanks, Will Smith and my favorite, Danny Trejo. All the top stars in Hollywood will be working on our lot, Ricardo," she said.

It was clear that Dolores would muscle her way back on top.

"I'll show those Hollywood moguls they can't abuse Ricardo and me. Together we'll make such good movies, everyone will come to see them," she proclaimed. "We'll build an empire so big, we'll put the other studios out of business. Those moguls will be sorry they chewed me up and spit me out. I'll destroy them."

After a week of kissing their check and conjuring up Hollywood-size pipe dreams, including all the Academy Awards their Dolric Pictures would win, the doorbell rang. Dozens of long-lost relatives from south of the border got wind of the windfall.

Like an army of blood-sucking vampires, their allegados descended on Dolores and Ricardo and sucked them dry.

Quizlet: Guess who's coming to dinner, and dinner, and dinner?

The Wrinkle Fairy

Word Count: 399
Reading Time: just over a minute 30 seconds

Everyone agreed that Prunella had the most beautiful complexion for a 70-year old: remarkable skin, unlined, rosy-cheeked and glowing.

Her friends asked what she did for her skin. "Absolutely nothing; I wash it, that's all."

What Prunella didn't tell anyone was that every night the Wrinkle Fairy paid her a visit. At the Wrinkle Fairy's request, Prunella would extract a drop of blood from her index finger with a lancet, one prick, never more. No questions asked. That's the way the Wrinkle Fairy wanted it, and that's the way it was for 40 years.

Prunella never knew what the Wrinkle Fairy did with the blood, nor did she want to know. All Prunella cared about was her peaches-and-cream complexion. Year after year the Wrinkle Fairy conducted her business, patted Prunella on the cheek and was off until the next nocturnal blood-letting.

Then one night when Prunella was 85-years old, the Wrinkle Fairy stopped coming. And she didn't come the next night or the night after that. Prunella's face developed forehead lines, crow's feet, bags under the eyes and a profusion of road-map lines all over her face. She even had a turkey wattle neck to go with it.

The formerly fair matron was out-of-her-mind crazy, upset that the Wrinkle Fairy had abandoned her when she needed her magic touch the most.

After that, Prunella didn't show her face outside her house. She became reclusive. She took to looking at herself in the mirror with the lights off. When friends knocked on her door, she didn't answer it. Prunella didn't want anyone to see her all wrinkly and dried up like a prune.

"I'd die to have my beautiful skin back," she told herself, as she cried herself to sleep. That night the Wrinkle Fairy returned. This time she wanted a tablespoon of blood instead of a drop.

"Why a tablespoonful?" Prunella asked innocently.

The Wrinkle Fairy whipped around and fired, "You dare to question me you rude, impertinent minion?"

"If you must know," the Wrinkle Fairy shot back, "facial rejuvenation is much harder for me than maintenance." She then gave Prunella a slap on the cheek and was gone.

A week later her friends all gathered around. Everyone agreed: "Prunella looked as beautiful now as when she was 20. It's amazing how her skin still glowed in the coffin."

Quizlet: Does the Wrinkle Fairy have an email address?

Big Stinky

Word Count: 627
Reading Time: two minutes 30 seconds

Madeline "Maddie" Phoenix was the proud possessor of a corpse plant, something rarely seen outside a botanic garden.

The huge plant had belonged to her mother and her grandmother before her, a living family heirloom. When it bloomed it had a ginormous flower, but the Phoenix family corpse plant had never bloomed.

Why the family kept it, they never said. The plant was big and ugly. In 80 years all it did was take up space, half the dining room.

But just like the Chicago Cubs and the pennant, hope sprang eternal with the Phoenixes. Finally, the behemoth bloomed: a single phallus of a shoot that shot straight up four and a half feet in the air.

Maddie called her friend, Kalavit Diddlysquat, an Israeli/ English horticulturist, to stop by and take a look.

"Come over right away," said Maddie, and bring a clothespin. "Big Stinky is going to kill me.

Diddlysquat's claim to fame was bringing the heaven/ hell/purgatory theme-garden, design concept to America from France, where she saw it at the Chateau de Miserey Garden in Giverney. She enjoyed traveling the country telling clients what they could do with their angel's trumpets, love lies bleeding and devil's darning-needles.

But for now, Kalavit was all about preventing a panic attack. She rushed over to the house smelling of death. What she saw was an erotic-looking plant growing in an old wash tub smelling up Maddie's place.

Maddie was wearing a surgical mask. "I can't breathe," she said. "I'm suffocating."

"Calm down, Maddie." said her friend. "It's all right."

Flies were beginning to land on the frilly-edged, purple base of the plant and crawl around in the four-foot wide, cup-like bottom of the flower capsule, the horticulturist observed. Then, more flies started filling the room, drawn by the fetid odor of rotting flesh from the sulfur-laden fumes Big Stinky was pumping out.

"Get this garbage can of a plant out of here," yelled Maddie."I don't want it anymore. Get rid of it. I hate it. Set it on fire."

"Don't talk nonsense," said Kalavit Diddlysquat."Your Amorphophallus is a botanic wonder. And hasn't it been in your family for three generations? Once it stops blooming it won't stink anymore."

"Amorpho, who cares? Take it away. Take it away." Maddie screamed.

After she put her friend Maddie to bed, Kala rounded up two husky teenage boys to move the plant to Maddie's patio.

"You mean that big thing in the rusty tub?" asked the one kid. "It smells like my gym socks."

"A lot worse," said the other kid.

"Boys, please, I'll give you something if you move it," Kala told them.

So they did. Or tried to. Big Stinky wouldn't budge. Everyone was feeling sick. Kala opened all the windows and doors. More flies streamed into the house.

They needed another pair of hands, but Kalavit Diddlysquat wasn't about to get a hernia, so she snagged another teen practicing football in the park across the street.

"Just move it," she said. "I'll take care of you boys."

The three boys huffed and groaned, gagged, and sweated their way out the door with Big Stinky.

Kala tossed each teenager a mini-size Snickers from a bag she found laying on the kitchen counter.

She Fabreezed the house and went home.

Hours later Kala came over to see if Maddie had recovered.

"Where's Big Stinky?" Kalavit asked. 'It's not on the patio."

"Don't know," replied Maddie.

"How could it disappear?" asked Kala, "it weighed a ton."

"The garbage men must have hauled it away," Maddie said.

The next day the news channel reported that a plague of flies enveloped the city dump and formed a black cloud of biblical proportions.

Quizlet: Can you kids move my grand piano? I'll take care of you!

17

Maris The Heiress

Word Count: 397
Reading Time: just over a minute 30 seconds

Maris Harris had a good life with not a care in the world. Why would she? Maris was the heiress to a candy company that had been around for generations, rated one of the tops in the world.

Recession-proof Oowegoey Corporation turned out everything from thin, delicate ribbon candy to pecan logs, to licorice whips and peppermint sticks, and much, much more. In the last few years, the company added gummy candy to its line.

Gummies were a huge success except for one stumble, when Oowegoey had a market failure with fish-shaped gummies that contained a drop of fish oil for authenticity. It was the aftertaste that sunk sales.

Maris the heiress worked for the family business for a while. Her daddy put her in customer service where all she heard were complaints from customers that the company's candy made them fat and rotted their teeth. Longsuffering Maris was polite; she empathized, apologized and gave them coupons for more candy.

Through her efforts, Oowegoey developed a candy that actually had a slimming effect and at the same time contained xylitol, a sugar said to prevent cavities. Sweet Thins, a 25-calorie chocolate, caramel, peanut butter introduction was the legacy Maris the heiress left for posterity.

After she retired from the company business at age 30, Maris spent her life in idleness, but even that became boring. The heiress took up art. She was inspired by the rolled, concentric circles of artist Wassily Kandinsky which reminded her of pinwheel candy.

She invented the candy collage, a less-than-fine-art that needed only a large supply of assorted candy and edible glue to produce portraits of famous and not-so-famous people. Her motto: "If you don't like it, eat it!"

The candy heiress was invited to hang her candy collages at libraries and schools, but soon learned those probably weren't the best of venues, because kids would stop by, pop off a mini marshmallow from Elvis' jumpsuit or snack on a Muppet and ruin it. And what's a Donald Trump with a balding head?

Luckily, Maris had an unending supply of free, Oowegoey candy to repair or create masterpieces making her art affordable, if not enduring.

Unfortunately, buyers turned their backs on her creations when they discovered her candy collages attracted bugs. Maris never sold another one again.

Moral of the story: Candy is dandy, unless you have worms in your Wassily

Easy Money

Word Count: 374
Reading Time: a minute 30 seconds

Maris Harris, the candy heiress, cruised through the drive-thru at Mickey D's in her Alfa Romeo when she spotted an Egg McMuffin wrapper under the drive-up window. Because she didn't appreciate littering, Maris opened her door to retrieve it. When she did, she noticed change on the pavement below the window. She went back at night and saw it still there, so she scooped it up, $1.98 cents!

Just for kicks, Maris the heiress dropped by the drive-up at another burger joint and discovered 79 cents more. The next week Maris checked out all the drive-thrus in the neighborhood. On a good day, she got five or six bucks. Maris the heiress was on a roll, so she expanded her rounds to include banks, where the collection from people who missed the drive-up drawer was even better. She justified her pilfering by telling herself, "If it's still there after closing, they don't want it."

One day, Maris strolled up the street, looked down at the pavement and found a quarter. She turned a corner near the city's big hotel and casino, and the wind hit her in the face with a $20 bill. Now she was on to something. Easy money all over the place. Maris the heiress didn't need it, but she liked it and snagging it became an obsession.

Later she noticed a half dollar sticking out of the soil in the planting of a downtown building. Maris brought a spoon from home and started digging. She invested in a metal detector and shovel and began digging around another old building. It looked like a gopher took up residence.

Her hard work paid off. Maris unearthed a treasure: a stash of old, gold coins that must have been buried there since the 1800s.

What a find! It was worth millions! Maris' lucky day! Imagine, right there, two feet under and just outside the federal building. Maris was so intent on digging and scooping that she failed to see the cop standing above her.

Now Maris the heiress spends most of her time DOING time— three to five years more or less.

Moral of the story: If you're picking up easy money,
do it when the cops are at the donut shop.

The Girl Who Could Fly

Word Count: 589
Reading Time: just over two minutes 15 seconds

In her 60s, Skylar Flockhart took up flying like a bird on the wing.

It happened three years after her near-fatal downhill skiing accident when a tree refused to get out of her way. Skylar was left unable to walk and confined to a wheelchair.

Skylar began having dreams that she could fly, luxurious, awesome images that made her wake up in the morning feeling wonderful.

At first, she had them every couple of months then more frequently. She longed for more freedom-enhancing flying dreams and the feeling of abandonment they provided.

One night, Skylar said her prayers and eased into bed wishing she'd have visions of being able to fly. In the darkness, Sky found herself standing by her wheelchair. This was no dream. She knew it was real. Skylar settled down into her wheelchair, then stood up carefully on her wobbly legs, took a tentative couple of steps then felt secure. Sky could walk! Hard to believe but true. Just like that. She also could hardly believe what happened next.

Sky stood up very straight, pushed off from the wheelchair, leaned back and elevated about three feet off the ground. After practicing until the sun came up, she could fly comfortably around the room, around the apartment and around the neighborhood.

Flying was exhilarating, life-transforming and puzzling. She flew over to her sister's house because Emily had to be first to see this, but Emily wasn't home. Skylar went out on the street and flew past a jogger, but the jogger didn't notice.

"Look up, look up," Skylar called, but the jogger wore headphones so he couldn't hear her. Skylar wanted to rip the jogger's headphones off, and say, "Look at me," but then she spotted a neighbor and honed in on her.

The neighbor opened her mailbox, and Skylar rushed to display herself, but the woman grabbed her bills and headed back inside.

"What good is it to fly if nobody sees me?" Sky asked herself.

Still, it was strange that others were so preoccupied they didn't notice her. "They probably don't even notice the clouds in the heavens, the mountains or the ocean," she said to nobody in particular.

Skylar flew by the strip mall and hunted for Emily without success in the drugstore, the post office and the grocery store.

When Sky couldn't find her sister, she decided to take a trip to nearby San Francisco where the Chinese New Year Parade was in progress. She'd always wanted to go there, and Skylar found herself IN the parade perched high atop a fire-breathing dragon float. What fun! People waved but were they waving and shouting at her?

On the way home, Sky stopped at the ocean and played with the dolphins. Back above ground, she shared the airspace with a flock of geese who surveyed her inquisitively.

"At least they noticed if no one else did," she remarked.

Back home, Skylar headed for her sister's house again.

"Em's got to be home by now," she said to herself. "I can't wait to amaze her."

When Sky got there, she saw Emily in tears. Her sister was talking to their pastor, Father Hofnagle.

"And what hymns have you selected for the funeral Mass, Emily?" asked the priest.

"Oh, what's that one?" Emily replied, mumbling through her tears. "Skylar was very fond of the words. It goes, 'and He will raise you up on the last day'."

Moral: If you find yourself flying, check your pulse to see if you're still alive.

Jail Break

Word Count: 243
Reading Time: just under a minute

Halcy waited impatiently for the arrival of her husband with a birthday cake containing a concealed weapon. She entered the visitor's room to see a smiling David holding a carrot cake that said, "Happy Birthday, Lifer."

David was having a happy day himself because he framed his wife for the murder of his girlfriend, and he's getting away with it. He thought Halcy didn't know it, but she did.

He knew Halcy was planning a jail break he hoped failed, perhaps socking her with another 50 or so incarcerated years. David was more than happy to deliver the cake with a special decoration inside the layers. Go for it, Halcy!

"I told you devil's food!" Halcy shrieked. She pulled a goo-covered knife from the cake and lunged at David.

Or maybe not.

"I said devil's food!!!" Halcy pulled a goo-covered GUN from the cake and shot David.

Or not.

The jail guard checked the goofy, firecracker candle-lit cake for weapons. Halcy scooped up a hunk of carrot cake with her fingers. She poked the guard in the eyes, temporarily blinding him with cake icing and threw the cake at David, whose hair and face set on fire followed by his clothing.

"Devil's food!!!" Halcy bellowed as she bolted from the room. Alarms sounded. Halcy was riveted with bullets; she looked like she was wearing polka dots. Guards shot her dead as she tried to escape.

Moral of the story: Another lousy birthday.

The Church Lady

Word Count: 534
Reading Time: just under two minutes 15 seconds

Virgene Scrupelle attended services at Saint Betta B. Good Catholic Church where she made every day Judgment Day. She staked out her special place in the choir loft strategically positioned for optimal sin-watching.

When she spotted talkers from her perch, the church lady blasted the heathens with a gush of holy water; teens texting coming in or going out. Blast! She rained down justice on song book manglers. Blast! Eaters and drinkers: Blast! To thwart the tall people who sat up front and blocked the view, out of range for her water blaster, Virgene put hymnals in the pews so it looked like the seats were occupied.

The church lady kept handy wipes ready after shaking hands with the scrofulous during the highly-expected "Sign of Peace." She abhorred that unsanitary gesture of friendliness, often opting for a fist bump or a discreet restroom dash with a contrived cough. Virgene didn't realize there were more germy germs in the holy water font than she'd ever pick up shaking hands.

"Doesn't anyone come to church to pray?' church lady wondered as she checked on the other distracteds. Taking notes on moral scum who wore inappropriate clothing, pilfered from the lost and found box or committed other heinous deeds kept her lingering after services. She blocked "flee-ers" as they tried to leave church early with her "you're going to hell" look. Virgene spent so much time in church, visitors asked her to hear their confessions.

The church lady was happiest on trips to hospitals and nursing homes where she felt appreciated. She'd crank out a froggy rendition of *Amazing Grace* and accompany herself on the accordion. The sick folks loved it, especially those who were too sick to hear it.

It was a curious thing: anytime anyone was dying, Virgene seemed to appear out of nowhere with Last Rites leaflets to send them heaven-bound, along with a scapular, big-time, anti-hell, anti-anathema ammunition. To the terminal, the sight of the church lady showing up in their hospital rooms was like seeing the Grim Reaper.

One day, a reporter who had been trying to get an interview with Virgene Scrupelle for months, ran her down at the post office. She heard backbiters call Virgene, the Grim Reaper, but the reporter didn't give it a thought when she took Twitter, her parrot, along for the ride.

Virgene exited the post office and headed for her car as the reporter approached her. The wind caused a couple of handy wipes and holy cards to drop from church lady's coat pocket and flutter in the breeze.

The frightened Twitter may have thought a flock of osprey was coming to eat him, because the parrot flew out the window. He dived beneath the car and wouldn't come out until the church lady picked up her papers and drove off. After Virgene pulled out of the lot, it seemed like the parrot escaped the Grim Reaper.

The reporter lost interest in writing up Virgene, after Twitter flew out from under the car and promptly got hit by an incoming mail truck.

Moral of the story: Don't take your parrot to the post office when the Grim Reaper might be picking up her mail.

IT'S RAINING CASH!

Word Count: 751
Reading Time: three minutes

Chip Upham never dreamed what hell would rain down on him when he saw hundred dollar bills falling from heaven onto his backyard picnic table.

The afternoon started innocently enough with a gathering of his friends doing what they always did when the Green Bay Packers had a home game: enjoying a tailgate party in Chip's backyard, a stone's throw from Lambeau Field.

The first to notice the money floating down was Chip's army buddy, Lewnie Clooney, who was shocked to see a C-note land in his potato salad. Bart Barph noticed several bills splash down into his brewski, while the other old boys, Dolbie Goolby, Chuckie Pecorino and Captain Cod got so pumped, they started scooping up fistfuls of Franklins from the deck, the grass and everywhere else in the yard, even the grill where a dozen bills were charbroiling along with the hamburgers.

Barph, who had seen a bit of money in his decades-ago career as a ball player, remarked that there must be millions raining down. Barph welcomed ways he could use the cash, as did Dolbie Goolby, who bred Labrador Retrievers, Chuckie Pecorino who owned a Kaukauna cheese processing plant and Cap Cod, a fishing guide.

Since Chip was the money man, he held the cash for safekeeping while he figured out how the windfall got there and how they could keep it.

The next day, Chip learned some bachelor named Rodney Blip won 12 million dollars in Vegas and was flying to India to fulfill a promise made to Mother Theresa's orphanage. Over Green Bay, Wisconsin, Blip and his money were lost when the plane burst into flames.

Because the millionaire had no relatives that laid claim to his estate, Chip waited six months to see if anyone came forward. And come they did—wolfish people sniffing around. In the days that followed, Chip was stalked by a pushy stockbroker, he ran off trespassers carrying shovels, he fended off a cat burglar and he got mugged on his way to work.

The shady tax accountant developed paranoia thinking that too many people had gotten wind of the little secret. Chip didn't want the IRS to know he alone was sitting on 12 mil. Since he was frazzled by the unwanted attention that had tailed him since the day the money fell from the sky, Chip divided the loot into six lots.

He rounded up his pals, and they agreed to his finders-keepers, no-tax scheme where they could share the money after seven years, provided each hid his portion from the IRS.

The money brought out repressed hostility in Bunny, Chip's wife, who felt left out when Chip parked his two million-dollar cut in a safe deposit box in his name only.

Chip's friends hid their stash in seemingly secure places but in the course of seven years, things changed. Lewnie Clooney rolled his up in an old rug in the attic, but his wife inadvertently sent it off to Goodwill.

Bart Barph hid his in a basement chest freezer, cold cash, as it were. But during a power outage years later, the Mrs. accidentally tossed out the cash along with rotting, defrosted elk, moose, and deer venison, some muskie, and a dead parakeet all wrapped in butcher paper.

Dolbie Goolby buried his dough in the backyard, but one of his pups dug it up, tore it to shreds and ate it. Chuckie Pecorino packed his cash in a wheel of cheese that needed a seven-year age, but mice got into the cheese plant, and you know the rest. Cap Cod rammed his two million in a metal, waterproof box in a secret fish crib on Lake Winnebagel, but a huge, high-speed cabin cruiser hit the fish crib one night. The box ripped open and the money fell to the bottom of the lake where the paper rotted in the muck.

At the end of seven years, the friends met in the safe deposit room of the bank to share the loot. One by one they reported on their disasters. The guys started fighting with Chip because they wanted to split Chip's share, since nothing else was left. But Chip was reluctant to share. He'd sooner lose his friends than part with any of his two mil.

On a tip from revenge-seeking Bunny, who was now pursuing a divorce, the IRS showed up. The feds confiscated the money and hauled Chip and his friends off to the pokey for tax evasion.

Moral of the story: Don't mess with the IRS.

The Oscar Party

Word Count: 370
Reading Time: a minute 30 seconds

At Polly Thigpen's memorial service, one of her best friends, Gloria Swansong gave a eulogy singing the praises of her boffo parties.

Gloria recalled a night several years back when guests watched the Academy Awards on TV. She thought of everything: a red carpet, swag bags for the guests, little chocolate Oscar statuettes covered with gold foil, voting ballots, production clap board napkins and placemats that featured a replica of the stars on the Hollywood Walk of Fame sidewalk, where guests could insert their own names.

Friends dressed as their favorite celebrities. Liberace, Sonny and Cher and Marilyn Monroe were among the stand-outs. Gloria Swansong was, who else, Gloria Swanson. She brought along a short bald-headed man who came as Max from *Sunset Boulevard*.

One clever woman, who someone called Rosanne Rosanneadanna because she resembled the Gilda Radner character, wore a gorgeous gold, strapless formal gown she picked up at a second hand store. She looked like the Oscar statuette.

And no Oscar party would be complete without a real Oscar on the guest list, Oscar Francken, impeccably garbed in a black tuxedo. Oscar hit the bubbly pretty hard that night. He staked out the punch bowl as it became replenished. He lingered long after the year's Best Film was announced on TV. A handful of guests stayed to make sure he was sober.

At midnight another guest took his car keys. At one a.m. the hostess suggested he stay the night. At two a.m. Oscar was found with his head buried in the punch bowl licking the bottom.

Then the most amazing thing happened. Oscar staggered to the front of the small group and grabbed her magic wand to use as a microphone, from a woman dressed as Glenda the Good Witch.

Francken was practically incoherent as he sputtered and mumbled into the wand, rocking back and forth in an attempt to stay upright, waving the wand about wildly. Eyes popped and chins dropped as onlookers watched as he became transfigured.

Oscar physically morphed into Oscar winner Lee Marvin's classic drunken bum from *Cat Ballou*.

Moral of the story: If you are called upon to give a eulogy, it's a good idea to at least mention the deceased.

Hide And Seek

Word Count: 175
Reading Time: just under 45 seconds

Night terrors woke Mary Ann Cross. She jumped out of bed screaming, as the result of a terrifying dream in which she lost the most important thing she ever owned, something irreplaceable.

Mary Ann hunted for a priceless treasure, more important than health or wealth, family, friends more important than life itself.

"IT'S GONE! IT'S GONE!" she wailed. "Better that I was never born." The woman didn't know what she was looking for, but in a panic, trashed the room for it, peering under the bed, ripping up the sheets, slashing pillows, tossing clothes about, pulling out drawers, searching her night stand, closet and shelves. She even checked under her wimple, laying in a crumpled heap in the corner.

Mary Ann, deprived of her sleep and her sanity, looked and looked with Messianic zeal until she dropped to her knees from exhaustion.

When the three a.m. chimes rang for vespers, through her tears it dawned on her. Sister Mary Ann was looking for her soul.

Moral of the story: Don't develop a bad habit.

THE GRASS IS ALWAYS GREENER

Word Count: 795
Reading Time: three minutes 15 seconds

Punky Keister and Freddie Fabio had a good thing going. They'd been friends for months, hanging out at the Senior Center where they played cards and got to know each other pretty well.

Sixty-nine year old Punky was portly, had bad hips, got around on a scooter and lived in senior housing. The owner of a small lighting assembly plant that employed 65, he had a fat retirement portfolio, but didn't live large because he was saving the big bucks for his kids.

Freddie was totally different: tall, well-built, strong, and muscular from a lifetime working as a trainer in gyms around town. Retired two years ago, he hadn't planned ahead and struggled along on little else but his Social Security checks. He came to the Senior Center to forget his troubles.

The guys always talked about how much better the other one's life was.

"If I had your body," Punky said, "I could get a girlfriend and go places with her. Women don't want me the way I am. They see me, the scooter, my butt hanging over the seat, and they run the other way. I'm lonely."

"What are you talking about?" replied Freddie. "If I had your life I could relax, live in peace and stop worrying. I could afford the best surgeons and get the hips fixed with money no object. I'd travel the world and stay at the Ritz. Ah, Paris, London, Rome! I'd call a gated community my home where women couldn't bother me all the time like they do now."

"All I hear is, Freddie, can you fix my kitchen cabinet?"

"Freddie, can you come over and trim a tree for me?"

"Women drive me crazy. They won't leave me alone," Freddie said.

"I'd love to have women drive me crazy," said Punky, 'but we can stop thinking about how you got it better than me, or I have it better than you because trading places is just a pipe dream and nothing more."

That night when Punky and Freddie dropped off to sleep at their respective homes, they happened to have a similar dream. Each man put on the other one's shoes.

Punky woke up to a new, fit body. He gloried that women wanted him around. He was happy to be wanted, to be needed to be helpful to other people.

Out on his first date in years, Punky had feelings that hadn't surfaced in eons. His heart was pumping, his spirits were lifted, but he dropped off his date right after dinner because he didn't feel well. Every time after that when he took out a woman and got excited, the same thing happened.

Punky was so upset with Freddie, as he saw his dreams of love and happiness disappear, that his heart pounded much harder, with anger and frustration building up. Punky had tremendous chest pains and was taken to the hospital. It turned out Freddie had congestive heart failure and never told Punky.

That's a death sentence!" raged Punky. "If I get out of this hospital, I'm going to kill Freddie." But the angrier Punky got, the more erratic his ticker became, and the doctors began to worry.

Meanwhile, Freddie was dealing with Punky's old body. He couldn't stand being confined to a wheelchair. He started having leaking accidents. Evenings were lonely and painful. His hips hurt all the time. Doctors refused to operate, saying he was a poor surgical risk.

"I can't live like this. I can't fly like this. I can't travel the world. I can't go very far from home. The farthest I can travel is the nearest bathroom," Freddie told himself.

"What good is all the money in the world, when I can't lead a normal life? I'm going to shoot myself," said Freddie, "but not before I shoot Punky first. How dare he keep these deal-breakers from me?"

The next day at the Senior Center Punky and Freddie confronted one another. They got into a terrible fight that caused fear in those that came for lunch.

"You didn't tell me you had CHF," screamed Punky.

"You didn't tell me you had OAB," yelled Freddie.

"DVT!"

"COPD!"

ABCDEFG—back and forth they rankled.

The place cleared out fast, as Punky threw a knife that narrowly missed Freddie, and Freddie pulled a gun. The cops hauled off the two seniors for disorderly conduct and disturbing the peace.

His alarm clock broke the silence in Punky's apartment; he woke up looking at his trusty scooter.

Freddie woke to a woman knocking on his door to come give her car battery a jump.

Both could only thank their lucky stars for their respective lives as they lived them.

Moral of the story: Don't go to the Senior Center to play cards.

Flora

Word Count: 536
Reading Time: just under two minutes 15 seconds

Flora was fresh from the shelter for victims of sex trafficking.

It had been a rough year for the girl. She had just finished high school when she lost her parents in a plane crash, along with her hopes of going to college and becoming a social worker.

Shortly thereafter, Flora went jogging and made a life-altering decision to stop when two men in a car waved her down for "directions." They snatched her, and when she woke up she was the latest casualty of the sex trade.

Flora would rather forget the agony and desperation of the following months. As rescuers raided the house where she was being held as a sex slave, hope sprang anew in her young heart.

The last few months of safety, kindness, nutrition, counseling and validation had gone far to spur the healing process and scare away the bad dreams that haunted her sleep. The day finally arrived when Flora could leave the safe house and begin a normal life on her own. She was in a good place and happier than she had been for a while.

The staff saw her off with nice, used clothes and shoes, a bag of personal items, a boxful of groceries and useful items and an all-inclusive scholarship to the state university, courtesy of a generous benefactor. Flora picked up the pieces of her shattered life and moved on, thanks to a world of support, caring and big-hearted people.

The next morning in her one-room apartment, she made her first home-cooked meal in a long time. One of the useful items the shelter sent along was a can opener and the other, which immediately became her prized possession, a frying pan someone had donated to the shelter. It was new, shiny and non-stick, and you'd think it was an antique treasure the way she 'pan-handled' it.

Flora pulled out a carton of eggs from her mini-frig and a can of corned beef hash from the bag of groceries. She remembered how her mother used to make corned beef hash for her, and how she loved it.

The girl put her precious pan on the hot plate and watched the corned beef and eggs sizzle as she grabbed a paper plate and plastic fork. It smelled awesome, and she could hardly wait to eat this grand meal.

Flora took one, big bite and moved toward the single chair and small table in her apartment where she could luxuriate over her royal breakfast. Startled by a noise in the hall, Flora dropped the paper plate. As she did, eggs and hash went flying and landed on the rug.

The new college student looked sadly at her ruined meal. It was the only can of hash in the bag.

"I might not get anymore to eat," she said, falling back on old patterns of doubt and fear.

But Flora was a survivor. She just made it through torture. She wasn't going to let a mishap like this dampen her spirit.

Then, without further hesitation, she got down on her hands and knees, spooned up the hash and licked the runny eggs off the rug with her tongue. Booyah!

Moral of the story: Count your blessings!

Dare Devil

Word Count: 309
Reading Time: a minute 15 seconds

Rod McQueen had a dull and boring job as a cost accountant, so in his spare time he engaged in exciting and adventurous sports and recreation. He liked the thrill of living on the edge and loved skydiving, zip lining and bungee jumping. The wannabe Evil Knievel raced cars, boats and commuted to work on a Harley.

The dare devil gouged out a piece of his knee with the knee cap exposed and walked a mile for help when he ran his motorcycle on slippery, wet leaf-covered terrain. He had scars on his scars. Rod developed bruises on a weekly basis, so many bruises people thought they were tattoos. The guy was otherwise fit, healthy and ate right so that nothing happened to him that did lasting damage.

His friends shook their heads and wondered why Rod did such perilous things. Flirting with danger was fun, got his juices going and made him happy, and he in turn made others happy. People liked him, and he had many friends.

But Rod always had a nagging uneasiness in the back of his mind.

When he was in his 20s, he said, "I'm not going to live to 30."

When he was 30, he said, "I'm not going to see 40."

When he was 40, he said, "I won't make it to 50."

After his 50th birthday, Rod stopped making ridiculous assumptions about his demise and never talked that kind of nonsense again. Once he put his demons to rest, he relaxed and took life in stride. He finally reasoned he was going to live a very long, long time.

At 60, Rod McQueen strolled through a quiet meadow one afternoon and leaned down to smell a flower. He got stung by a bee and died there of anaphylactic shock.

Moral of the story: Stay aware from danger—avoid meadows.

CRAB

Word Count: 732
Reading time: just under three minutes

Rocky, a musician, and Lola, the singer in his band, flew from Jersey down to Boca to spend the weekend at their beach house. The couple needed a respite from the clamor and stress of the bar where they performed.

The two had a great time relaxing in the sun and sipping tequila when a dark cloud began forming around Rocky. Something piddly ticked off Rocky; the couple gathered their towels and suntan lotion and took the argument inside.

Rocky barked at Lola for no reason at all. It might have been something he ate earlier at the tiki bar. (Those 'appy' hour appetizers sat out in the heat far too long.) Or maybe it was the ulcer medicine he forgot to pack. That often meant Rocky belched fire.

The band leader carried on for what seemed to be a long discordant score. Rocky couldn't stop, and Lola couldn't stand it. When she told him, "enough, already," and offered him a glass of milk, it made him even madder. Rocky knocked the glass of milk from her hand sending a spray of liquid at her. That was it! Lola felt he was stomping on her, and she couldn't breathe. She walked out— no shoes, no purse, just the shorts and the milk-wet tank top she was wearing.

It was late now; she had been walking the beach for hours. Lola wanted to get as far away from her loud-mouthed husband as she could. With no full moon to illuminate the beach, she stumbled over a turtle. She turned the turtle right side up and said to him, "How many times do I have to go through this? He's always yelling."

When it began raining and her bare feet started hurting, Lola headed back. She took a safer way home along an illuminated, wooden boardwalk. She spied a bait shop on the boardwalk with a bench outside and sat down to rest. Lola felt better now but cold, wet and tired.

In a flash, a bolt of lightning hit a large tank of fiddler crabs on which Lola was leaning. It was so close the impact knocked her to the ground along with several 100 crabs. She gently brushed away the crabs crawling all over her. The little creatures scuttled toward the sand and safety. Lola saved one crab for a pet, and as the thunderstorm intensified, she ran back to the beach house.

When she got there she crumpled into a chair, shivering. Immediately, Rocky was on her.

"What's wrong with you? Are you so stupid you stay out in the rain? You want to catch pneumonia, you dumb broad?"

Lola tried to distract Rocky, so she pulled the crab out of her pocket.

"Why did you bring that thing in here?" he roared.

With that, he grabbed it, threw it on the floor and was about to smash it, when Lola put her hand over the crab and he stomped on her fingers instead. Lola started crying, and Rocky went to the frig to get himself a beer. Exhausted, she seized the opportunity to crash on the couch. Rocky downed his beer, hit the sheets and quickly fell asleep. After she knew he was out, she slipped into her side of their bed.

Halfway through Rocky's REM cycle, the beach creature that had taken cover under their bed crawled slowly upward and made its way to Lola's pillow, still wet from her crying. The small crustacean saw Lola's swollen eyelids and crept slowly to the side of the bed where the musician slept. Rocky was a shameless mouth-breather, and the fiddler crab climbed over Rocky's shoulder headed toward the large orifice that was Rocky's mouth.

(What's scarier than the unseen, unknown, unwanted when it's crawling on you in the dark?)

The one-inch fiddler crab kept advancing and startled the musician who woke up. Rocky's bellow startled the fiddle crab too, and it pinched Rocky hard on the lip and tongue.

The crabby man ran around the room screaming with the little guy hanging on his tongue. Rocky tried to pull it off, but it wouldn't let go. The crab then moved further into Rocky's mouth, back into the recesses. Finally, with a last pinch to his vocal chords, the crab slipped down Rocky's throat. Presumably, Lola didn't hear Rocky suffocate. Presumably.

Moral of the story: All's well that ends well.

Ouch!

Word Count: 504
Reading Time: two minutes

When her baby teeth fell out Mona Mesial had good luck with the tooth fairy. When her permanent teeth came in Mona stopped getting quarters and started getting cavities.

Dr. Hurt called it "rampant decay." Mona's teeth rotted faster than you can say "peanut brittle." Mrs. Mesial was stuck driving her daughter to the dentist weekly. Mona's father worked two poorly-paying jobs just to keep up with the war being raged in his daughter's mouth.

Mona's folks were clueless as to why she had so many cavities. They were strict vegans with no sugar allowed in their home. Little did they suspect that their daughter had a sweet tooth that she hid from them. The little girl couldn't fight her big, ominous demon. It was like trying to deflate the Goodyear blimp with a pin. To satisfy her cravings, Mona begged neighborhood grocers for sweets and spent her allowance on Milk Duds and Charleston Chews. She had a secret stash of candy, so she never ran out.

In middle school, Mona traded lunches with the kids whose lunch boxes held goodies. By the time she started high school, Mona had six fillings in every tooth and had undergone three root canals. She held the Guinness Book of World Records for the youngest person ever to develop serious gum disease. Dr. Hurt said that by the time she was 20, Mona would not have a tooth left in her mouth.

Her father, Stan, was having his own problems. He was experiencing career failure. By the time his daughter started high school, he tried 15 different jobs, none of them fulfilling. Stan Mesial changed directions again and became a dentist because of his daughter's ongoing dental problems and mounting bills that choked the family finances. Mona's father went back to school; he enrolled in an online college program. Finally, Stan had found his niche.

The first job in his new career was as a temp dentist with a placement service. That very morning Mona lost the veneer on her front upper tooth after chomping down on a caramel apple during college freshman orientation. She rushed to visit Dr. Hurt who couldn't see her but offered help from another dentist in the office. Mona discovered that her father was the man with the drill in his hand. He was filling in for Dr. Hurt's colleague, off work with carpal tunnel woes.

Mona had no desire to be the first patient ever for a dentist fresh out of online dental school, let alone be a guinea pig for her father. But she was caught in a bind, so she just closed her eyes, opened her mouth and sucked it up.

As Stan Mesial wrapped up his awkward, heavy-handed drilling, something happened that can only be described as a volcanic eruption. One by one, Mona's teeth starting falling out of her mouth.

In the end, the 18-year old didn't look half bad with false choppers.

Moral of the story: If you see your father with a drill, run.

SPRING BREAK

Word Count: 798
Reading Time: just under three minutes 15 seconds

Dottie Dewright was supremely favored with a high-rise condo on the shimmering Gulf of Mexico. She and her late husband, Jonah, acquired the place 20 years ago as a Florida vacation getaway during their working years and a retirement home thereafter. They never dreamed a freak fishing accident with a marlin, that skewered Jonah straight through his gut, would take Jonah's life before he got the golden handshake.

The widow Dewright felt a blessing like a Florida beachfront condo was meant to be shared. She invited friends and relatives who were ill, suffered losses or needed a boost of some kind to spend a week or two at her condo.

The minute Dottie read in the backhome paper that the bishop of the diocese had fallen and broken his hip, she called the chancery office and offered her condo for the bishop's R and R. Dottie told the bishop's secretary that her condo would give him a nice break from the vagaries of an uncertain Minnesota spring.

"It's a small place, 990 feet small, but it has a million-dollar view," Dottie said, selling the idea to the secretary. "Please extend my invitation to His Excellency."

51

The secretary returned the call quickly. The bishop had snapped up the offer, packed his sunglasses, a bottle of Advil and was booked on a flight leaving March 15 for his spring break.

Dottie panicked. She wasn't thinking when she tossed out the condo idea to the bishop.

She had only invited relatives and friends to stay there, never a celebrity and never a person as eminent as His Excellency. "What's wrong with me? Why did I invite him?" she asked herself. "This place is not good enough for someone as important as the bishop. It's small, it's old, it needs that picture of dogs playing cards replaced with an icon, and I've only got a week until he gets here."

Dottie quickly set about making the most of what she had, with plans to showcase her humble condo as inviting, comfortable and welcoming. She installed new carpeting, painted the walls and bought new deck chairs. She hired a cleaning service and took the curtains to the cleaners. Now the place looked good, but not good enough. It must be perfect for the bishop.

"He can't eat off these chipped dishes," Dottie said. She ordered online from Crate and Barrel and requested priority overnight Fed Ex. "He can't sleep on these raggedy sheets. Hello Bed Bath and Beyond, throw in some towels and washcloths, and a shower curtain too."

"Looking great," she told herself.

The day before her most important guest ever was expected, Dottie readied for a final white glove test of her sparkling, adorable little condo.

But first she got down on her hands and knees. She spotted a tiny spider running for dear life. She noticed the cleaning people didn't do the job the way she'd have done it, so she grabbed a mop, pail and a toothbrush for the corners as a last-minute fixup. She scrubbed and wiped and slopped water all over.

Her plan was to make the condo bishop-ready, take a shower, pack up and drive back to Minnesota the following day, while the bishop and his hip limped around the beach for the next two weeks. Too bad she wouldn't be here to get to know him better.

She was disheveled, sweaty, smelly, with hair dripping wet. Still holding the wet mop, she responded to a knock on the door. The woman was horrified to see the bishop standing there. Without thinking, and fraught with exhaustion she said, "You're a day early," and slammed the door in the bishop's face.

Immediately she realized what she had just done and opened the door quickly. Here was the most important clergyman in northern Minnesota. It was like offending God. He was still standing there. The sweat dripped off her nose. Dottie couldn't talk.

"Hello, my dear," the bishop said warmly, it's so nice to see you again. I'll stay at the Holiday Inn down the street for the night, and in the morning if you are so disposed, I invite you to have breakfast with me."

The diplomatic bishop turned and headed calmly toward the elevator, whistling softly, as if what just happened never happened.

Inside Dottie dropped her smelly self into the nearest chair.

"I'll never forget this as long as I live," she told herself. Dottie was never so embarrassed in her life as right now."If only he had come on Saturday."

Then Dottie Dewright happened to glance at the calendar on the wall. "It WAS Saturday. It WAS March 15th. The only one who was a day off was Dottie.

Moral of the story: If you don't know what day it is, ask a bishop.

Trick Or Treat

Word Count: 621
Reading Time: two minutes 30 seconds

Patsy arrived at the Florida condo for her annual weekend and looked forward to seeing her now and again friends. They texted a month before about going bar-hopping and checking out the costume contests, popular at beach bars on Halloween.

Bummer! Now everybody had other plans. The Halloween junkie wasted a month for nothing making her bird costume.

Patsy went down to the pool area, but the security guard was locking it up for the night.

"Hey, don't lock the pool. I'm mad as hell, and I want to cool off. My friends let me down. I've got nobody to go bar hopping with me. Just give me a quickie, please?" begged Patsy.

"Can't help you with the pool; it's time to lock up," said the security guard, "but I could help you out with the other."

"Really? You'll take me to the bars? You'll do that for me?" asked the excited Patsy. "But I don't even know you, know your name. And don't you have to watch the condo complex?"

"I'm Randy, and I'll be here for a couple of weeks. I'm the fill-in security guard from the agency while Jack is on vacation. I could time out early, no big deal. "It's alright," said the security guard.

Randy was a tall, dark, handsome hunk, about half Patsy's age, the kind of looker any 64-year old gal would be thrilled to show off at the beach.

"Isn't that a wedding band on your finger?" asked Patsy, skeptically.

"Yeah, but my wife doesn't mind," Randy said, "she's used to me taking care of older gals and coming home late."

So even though Patsy felt a little uncomfortable with the situation, she felt worse about missing a good time.

"Give me 15 minutes to change into my costume," said Patsy, "and do you need some kind of outfit to wear?"

"I'll just go as a security guard," he said.

Randy pulled up to the entrance, Patsy jumped in the car, and a few minutes later they were at their first stop. The costume contest was over, but Patsy bought Randy a drink anyway. He took her to Nobody's Inn, another bar, another drink on Patsy, and they danced and watched the contest.

"This contest is a little lame, and their prizes are chinchy. Let's drop by "Never Goes Well," Patsy suggested. "Never has the best costume party on the beach and the prizes are awesome: a grand for first, $500 for second, and a whole slew of free drink coupons after that. They give out the prizes just before closing, so we're not too late."

"You're the boss," said Randy, "whatever you want."

"Randy, you're great to do this for me. Are you sure your wife doesn't mind you staying out all hours of the night?" asked Patsy.

"Nah, she wants me to do it. She does it too." laughed Randy.

"Ha, ha, ha, then let's make a toast to your wife," laughed Patsy.

When they got to Never Goes Well and her unique, hand sewn pigeon costume didn't even win a free drink coupon, she ordered Randy, "Take me back to the condo. I'm not amused anymore, and besides I'm feeling a little light-headed."

"You got it, honey," said Randy.

Once back home, Randy followed her up to her condo, loosening his shirt on the way.

"You still want that quickie?" he asked, "I've got time."

"What?" Patsy shot back. She thought he was just a nice guy helping her out because her friends dropped out.

"If you don't want it," Randy said, "I'll just take $50 an hour, instead of my regular $100!"

Moral of the story: Never dress as a pigeon on Halloween, especially if you're a patsy.

Toupe

Word Count: 371
Reading Time: a minute 30 seconds

Phil the barber was in the business a long time when something unusual happened.

Harry Crooks, a regular, rushed into Phil's shop early one morning.

"Phil, I've got to be in court in three hours and the dog got hold of my hairpiece. I can't be seen in public without it. There's slobber all over it, and the thing smells like skunk. There's an extra Franklin in it for you if you can fix this mess quickly."

"Sure, no problem, Harry," Phil reassured the lawyer, "since you're such a good customer, I'll make room for you, even though we're swamped today."

Crooks dropped his rug off and said, "Call my paralegal, Sue Yoo, the minute the hairpiece is ready, and we'll send a courier to pick it up."

Phil made good money cutting men's hair, but the toupe styling part of his business was even more lucrative.

For Harry, Phil would take charge himself. It didn't take long to trim, wash, and blow dry the piece then into the convection oven to set the style.

When Phil went to take it out of the oven, the toupe was fried.

"Who touched my oven?" Phil fumed. "The temperature is supposed to be on low at all times."

"I'm sorry, Phil," said Trixie, one of his funeral home stylists. "I turned the oven on high to make a pizza, and I forgot to turn it down again to low. I know I'm not supposed to use your oven, but I was pressed for time, and..."

"Well, Trixie," Phil said, trying to control his rage, "if you can figure a way out of this, I won't fire you," and the boss walked away.

Quick-thinking Trixie came back in five, offering, "we could switch rugs. Here's one I worked on last night that isn't due for pickup yet. It's the same color and style as Mr. Crook's. I'll go to the supply house on lunch break and pick up a replacement.

"You just saved your skin," said Phil.

The barber never told the lawyer that he was wearing a corpse's toupe, and Harry never knew the difference.

Moral of the story: Dead men tell no tales.

THE MAGIC FISH

Word Count: 761
Reading Time: three minutes

Joe Bub owned a run-down rowboat rental and bait shop, a dirty, smelly depressing place. His business was bad, he was unhappy, irritable all the time, with large warts all over his face, full of aches and pains and most of the time his life was drudgery.

One day, Walleye Wally, a local fisherman, rented one of Joe's decrepit boats and cheerfully went out on the water. When he returned, Joe noticed the guy left a large fish in the bottom of the boat.

The silvery fish sparkled in the sunlight. It was so beautiful, it lifted Joe's spirit. He had never seen a fish like this one, so he took its picture. Not one to waste anything, Bub retrieved the fish because it was still alive and flapping around. He cleaned it, cooked it and ate it. It was the best fish he'd ever tasted.

Joe perked up after he ate the fish; he began to feel better. In the next few days he even looked better. Younger! Attractive! Joe Bub believed the fish was magical. People heard about the remarkable change in the man, and his business picked up as the curious came around.

Soon more good things happened to Joe, as his new-found good looks attracted the woman of his dreams. They married and were happy. Fortune continued to smile on them and their boat rental and bait business.

Then, the fisherman returned, rented a boat from Joe and went out onto Lake Woodruff, this time with his son, looking for muskie. Again, Walleye Wally caught only one fish, another big one, but no muskie. This one looked different from the silvery-bellied one. It looked more like a catfish with barnacles. Wally returned the boat and tossed the smelly, old fish in the dumpster.

After the two left, Joe dived into the dumpster to retrieve the fish. He hoped this strange fish would bring more good luck and happier days still. Even though the fish was out in the sun too long, Joe choked down a good portion of it for luck. It made him sick. Joe was angry.

The next day, the large warts returned. Joe's looks faded, he got snarky, his help quit and people stayed away from his business. His wife left him because he was abusive, frightening, ugly and all his money was gone. Everything was going downhill in Joe Bub's life. He was worse off than before he ever met the fisherman and ate his lousy, magic fish.

As he saw his life slipping away, Joe tried a last-ditch effort to fix things. He took out one of his beat-up boats and tried to catch one of the silver-bellied fish that brought him so much luck the first time.

Out on Lake Woodruff, he caught many fish but threw them back because he was looking for one kind and one kind only. The game warden told Joe that both kinds of fish became extinct 100 years ago, but Joe knew that wasn't so because of Walleye Wally who left his catch behind.

While fishing, Joe saw Wally and his kid and asked where they caught the fish. Wally pointed to a channel which connected to Lake Content.

Joe was dead set on finding another silver-bellied magic fish. He needed a reversal of fortune. He needed a lifeline. His life had hit bottom. Joe headed for the channel and saw that it was pretty much impassable, even with his tiny rowboat.

Joe dragged the boat through the shallow water. It seemed like an eternity going through the channel. He was cold and sore, but Joe finally made it. Lake Content was sparkly, pristine and beautiful, the same Lake Content he remembered in good times when he was young.

Once on the water, Joe leaned over to get a minnow for his hook. When he looked up, he saw hundreds of large, silvery-bellied fish, just like the one Walleye Wally left in the rowboat, leaping out of the water like a beautiful ballet.

Joe was beside himself with joy. He flipped out. He knew that good fortune was almost within his reach. He saw himself feeling better, looking better, his business returning, his wife coming back to him, and then—

The fish jumped so wildly that one of them leaped into the rowboat, hit Joe in the head and knocked him out. Joe suffered a concussion that brought on amnesia. The warty, irritable, unhappy man had no recollection of magic fish or Walleye Wally.

Moral of the story: Gonna need a bigger boat.

MAGIC WHAT?

Word Count: 796
Reading Time: just under three minutes 15 seconds

"Remember me?" asked Walleye Wally.

Joe Bub, boat and bait shop owner and perennial loser, nodded but didn't have a clue who Walleye Wally was.

"We need a boat. Me and the kid are out for muskie," said the fisherman.

"They're out there," said Joe.

The fishing was lousy but Joe Bub didn't much care. Ever since his recent concussion, he had headaches that caused loss of interest in just about everything.

Soon, the headaches get so bad, he couldn't see straight. Joe went to the doctor and woke up in a hospital bed needing emergency brain surgery. To remove the brain tumor safely, doctors said they must sever nerves to either a part of the brain that controlled his sense of touch and feeling, or cut the nerves which led to the part of the brain which affected taste. The poor guy had to choose which sense was most valuable to him. Joe figured he could live without tasting another hamburger or chocolate bar, and after surgery, he went home and resumed his less-than-satisfying life.

Weeks later, Joe experienced excruciating pain in his skull and returned to the doctor, where he was told the brain tumor was aggressive and spreading toward the part of the brain that controlled not only the sense of touch and feeling, but the sense of smell as well. He had to decide again which sense to try and save; Joe chose his sense of smell.

Not long after, the brain tumor was back and growing out of control toward his ears. Did he want to save his hearing or his sense of smell? After choosing his hearing, Joe hit bottom. He was severely depressed and constantly moaned, "why, me?"

Doctors assigned a nurse, Carrie, to Joe who did double duty on suicide watch. She comforted him and brought him out of his self-destructive feelings. She helped him appreciate what he did have. Carrie was his only friend.

Soon, the two were enjoying long chats. She saw more than the sad soul who couldn't taste, feel or smell. She loved him warts and all. Carrie became Joe's everything. They fell in love.

Finally, his hearing went and then his eyes were threatened. Carrie helped Joe muster the courage for more surgery. When his last major sense was about to go, and Joe had trouble speaking, Carrie bought him a lucky lotto ticket for no apparent reason other than a distraction from his pain and overwhelming loss. The lotto ticket was indeed lucky.

Now Joe had enough dinero to spend the rest of his life in relative comfort. The joy of winning the lottery was diluted by the loss of his senses, but he began to see how really important the senses were in relation to wealth, as he struggled in his smell-less, feeling-less, tasteless, hearing-less, and nearly sightless, silent world.

With the help of his precious Carrie, Joe started to count his blessings, however few. He even embraced his losses, impossible as that seemed.

"You're so good to me," he told wrote on a slate. "I'm the luckiest guy in the world."

He was grateful for her loving care.

Joe scarfed down the fish she gave him for lunch, and within the hour, Joe could talk! He could see perfectly! He could see his beautiful Carrie, hear her dulcet voice, smell her perfume. There was no scientific explanation for it. It was a miracle!

Carrie moved to hold his hand and Joe felt it. Could Joe have died and gone to heaven?

Joe had never been so happy, so glad to be alive, so grateful to have his eyes, his nose, his ears, his hands, his mouth, things he never thought about when those parts worked before. And most of all Joe Bub was happy to have his kind, loving Carrie. He thanked a distant God, to whom he had never prayed.

"Do you believe in God?" Carrie asked Joe.

"I do now," Joe responded, as he kissed Carrie. Joe never felt like this before.

"Carrie, where did you get this fish?" Joe asked, as he swallowed the last bite.

"Oh, a man dropped it off," replied Carrie. "Said you would remember him as Walleye Wally and that he wanted you to have a hunk of the muskie he finally snagged."

Now it was all coming back to Joe: Walleye Wally, the magic fish, the concussion, everything.

He remembered he took a picture of the magic fish. "This is

just plain, old musky," said Joe. "This doesn't even look like the magic fish in the photo."

"Walleye Wally said to tell you there is no magic fish." said Carrie. "You are the magic, and the magic is the power within you to change!

Moral of the story: Eat more fish!

Get 'Uppa'

Word Count: 378
Reading Time: a minute 30 seconds

Following a car accident, Minerva McGroggy's doctor told her she was paralyzed for life. Minerva was bedridden. The news seemed grim, but still the disabled woman had a sweet life for an invalid.

That's because Minnie was a woman of means, filthy rich thanks to a lavish inheritance. She lived in a gorgeous mansion with a bedroom suite so expansive, it could swallow several tennis courts.

She conducted her life from her regal canopy bed, fit for a queen with satin sheets and a handmade goose down comforter. Everything was at Minerva's fingertips, including a staff of seven who catered to her every whim, even to the point where she sent a minion flying to New York for cheesecake, bagels and other frivolous indulgences.

Minerva had a master chef who whipped up gourmet entrees like Duck a l' orange and desserts including Baked Alaska. The lady of the house had a maid that groomed her and took care of her personal needs, also a housekeeper, a gardener, a dog walker, a personal shopper and a secretary.

Life was effortless. Minerva read 10 books a week, listened to Chopin and Rachmaninoff for hours, cuddled her two Pembroke

Welsh Corgis in the huge bed and spent endless time watching travel shows and soaps on her 80-inch wall-mounted TV.

Minnie indulged her fancy by playing the stock market; her broker made house calls. She remained close to her friends by spending hours a day texting them. She wanted for nothing.

One night, when the staff was sleeping and she wasn't, Minerva tried something daring. She slipped out of bed just to see if she could. It had been several years since the invalid had ventured from her room.

Minnie was amazed that she could walk and move like a normal person. She wasn't paralyzed at all. Now she could live her life like everyone else. She realized she could groom herself, fix her own hair, prepare her meals, clean her house, wash her clothes, work in the garden, walk her dogs, buy groceries and wait in endless lines at checkout counters.

"How dreadful," she thought.

With that, Minerva McGroggy dived back into bed and stayed there, where she lived happily ever after.

Moral of the story: Beware of bed sores!

Vocation

Word Count: 389
Reading Time: just over a minute 30 seconds

Her parents named her Scholastica to honor the patroness of vocations, hoping their little girl would become a nun. For as long as she could remember, little Tica wanted to become one too.

The girl got no encouragement from her brothers, unless jibes like "lock her up" and "put her away" count. The nun thing fizzled when Tica got swept off her 'feeta' by Archie Tarrier, a postal inspector, who charmed her with stories of cobras, tarantulas, larvae, guns, knives, explosives and toxic waste that crossed his path in the course of his work.

Recently, Archie was fired for taking his work home with him. Beer and wine are prohibited from shipment through the U.S. Postal Service. Now Archie just sits around the house gathering dust.

After 45 years of marriage and 24 grandchildren (or was it 25,) in Utah (or was it Idaho,) that old feeling welled up again inside Tica Tarrier.

"Would you mind if became a nun?" she asked her husband.

With a mouthful of popcorn, a sandwich and a beer in his hands, Archie was intent on watching the Cubs on the tube. He mumbled."Uh, uh, (or was it uh huh?") Tica couldn't tell and didn't care.

The 67-year old sister wannabe come-lately figured she had time on her hands to spare, because low maintenance Archie never left the couch. He required her services only to provide a sandwich and beer every so often and a refill on the popcorn bowl at snacktime.

Tica Tarrier, in the eleventh hour of wishful thinking, wrote a letter to the bishop, and though she wasn't a practicing Catholic, asked him if any orders of sisters might take her. She wanted to work out some kind of a deal. So she posed the suggestion of a dual vocation in her letter, questioning if perhaps some convent could use her part time, and the rest of the time she could stay put. A week later she got the bishop's reply.

His letter said only, "Are we having trouble at home, dear?"

"Oh well," Tica chuckled, "if the convent won't take me, perhaps I'll try to join the circus."

Moral of the story: Pray the Cubs win another World Series. Their chances are as good as being accepted in the convent or joining the circus at 67.

FAT CHANCE

Word Count: 725
Reading Time: just under three minutes

Tootsie Woll was a big girl, but she had a thing about weighing over 300 pounds. She held firm at 299-1/2 pounds. It wasn't easy.

A visit with her physician, Dr. Coughlin Emfazema, turned ominous when he told the pretty, but well-upholstered woman that she had high blood pressure, and was "this far" from getting congestive heart failure, diabetes, edema, gout, and even, heaven forbid, fat girl's rash.

"You're flirting with disaster, Tootsie. Better lose weight before it's too late. Do something, and do it fast," said the doctor, who was a little porky himself. "Mark my words, YOU'RE FLIRTING WITH DISASTER." Tootsie's first thought was to change doctors.

Dr. Emfazema's tough talk scared her and jolted Tootsie big time. The Toots went home and cried, because dieting was hopeless. Over the years, she had tried every diet on the face of the planet, lost weight, but gained it all back and more.

Tootsie went to the gym anyway, trying yet again to lose weight. But the first time on the treadmill, Toots broke it. They revoked her membership, so she pounded the pavement instead. Running and eating 500 calories a day got her electrolytes out of balance and caused her to hallucinate. This clearly wasn't working.

As usual, the chubby chick took her mutt to the dog park. When it was time to go, she called for Buster but he didn't come. He never came back. The next day, Tootsie went back to the park looking for Buster to no avail. She sat on a park bench, thought about how she had hit bottom and started to cry.

A lady sat down beside her and asked, "What's wrong? My name's Donna Rhea, and yours? Maybe I can help?"

"No one can help me. I can't even help myself. My husband left me, I have no friends, even my dog ran away and my doctor says if I don't lose weight, I'll die." Tootsie couldn't stop crying.

"Honey, let me help," said Donna Rhea.

"You're going to get my husband back? My friends? My dog?" Tootsie smarted off.

"No, on the first two counts, but I might be able to get you another dog," said Donna Rhea. "Look, I know I can help you lose weight and keep it off. How would you like to be wearing a size 10, looking 15 years younger, have the energy you had when you were a teenager and enjoy men salivating at the sight of you?"

"Fat chance," said Tootsie.

"I can promise you, I have the answer," Donna Rhea went on.

"I'm a researcher, and I've developed a miracle pill. With this pill, you never have to starve yourself again. You just live your life normally, and the pill takes care of everything. As He is my witness," said Donna Rhea looking up, "this is the answer to your prayers."

"What's in it?" Tootsie asked.

"I can't tell you. If it gets out, big pharmaceutical companies will snatch my formula, and I'll lose my competitive edge. But I guarantee, trust me, that if you don't see results in 90 days, I'll give you double your money back," she went on. "Just give me $150 and—"

"$150 dollars?" shrieked Tootsie. "You know how many Dunkin' Donuts I can buy with $150 dollars?"

"I know it's a lot," admitted Donna Rhea, "but your life is at stake. And don't you want to look gorgeous? One pill is all you'll ever need. You won't have to spend another dime on diet stuff. It pays for itself. And don't forget the money-back guarantee!" Donna Rhea could hardly spit out the words fast enough. "No exercising, no dieting, you eat whatever you please," added Donna Rhea.

"Even Dunkin' Donuts?" asked Tootsie.

"Even Dunkin' Donuts!" replied Donna Rhea. "What have you got to lose, except pounds?"

"Give it to me," said Tootsie.

Before long Tootsie began losing weight, 50 pounds the first three months, then 30 the next, and so it went, until she got down to a size 10.

But it didn't stop there. Tootsie continued to lose, down to 110 pounds, then 100, then 90, 85…down, down, down until one day the park police found a wallet with her ID in it and a pile of women's clothing laying in a puddle of water. That was all that was left of Tootsie Woll.

Quizlet: Does Dunkin' Donuts make munchkins?

Environment

Word Count: 337
Reading Time: just over a minute 15 seconds

Tetra was a little fish in a big pond, the ocean, while Goldie was a big fish in a small pond, an aquarium.

The little fish always feared he'd be eaten by a predator. He was super hyper, fleeing, darting and hiding. Almost every fish was a predator because tiny Tetra was barely hiccup size. Tetra hated living in the vast expanse of the ocean, but what could he do? That was his environment.

The big fish lived in a confined space in somebody's rec room. The people left on the lights day and night, so Goldie couldn't sleep. She ate very little fearing she would outgrow her environment. There was no place to hide. She bumped into the glass at the slightest noise, causing loss of beautiful, golden scales. Sometimes the kids in the family pounded on the aquarium which amplified sound inside to a deafening level.

Worse yet, Goldie shared the cramped space with three other goldfish that were growing at an alarming rate. Very soon there would not be enough room to move around, let alone turn around.

"Stop eating, stop eating!" she screamed, "You're going to kill us all. But the other goldfish paid her no mind.

Goldie was so unhappy her dorsal fin drooped. Hoping somebody would liberate her, Goldie jumped out of the aquarium when the dad sprinkled fish flakes on top the water. She landed on the rec room floor, flapping frantically and gasping for water. Nobody got her message.

It was the worse day of Goldie's sad life. The big goldfish was returned to her underwater torture chamber and never lived long enough to find freedom.

Meanwhile Tetra was swimming about nervously when a diver scooped him up. The little bitty fish was headed for a pet store and eventually a home where he'd find contentment, safety and nourishment in a huge aquarium provided by a conscientious owner, and home already to a few new friends, neon tetras like himself.

Moral of the story: Even fish have feelings!

THE BUG IN THE RUG

Word Count: 743
Reading Time: three minutes

"Hi! I'z Ozzie, what's yo name?" asked the bug in the rug. Fifth grader Mitchell Hally's eyes popped.

"What?" said the 10-year old. "You talking to me?"

"Sho nuf," said the bug.

The boy thought that maybe his cousin was playing a joke on him by hiding behind the drapes in the rec room, with a microphone hidden behind a chair.

But then he saw the little, brown bug in the deep pile, same color as the carpeting. The bug's tiny mandibles were moving, and his black, beady eyes were looking at Mitchell.

"I'z Ozzie, what's yo name?" the bug repeated.

Mitchell was dumbfounded.

"Jus' say yo name, boy," insisted the bug.

"M—M—Mitchell!"

"Yo live 'round here?" asked the bug.

"Yeah," Mitchell replied.

"Me too!" said the bug, "fo the las six munts."

The bug told the boy how he stowed away in a furniture delivery from the South, found the living here safe and warm, with bits of crumbs for the picking in the wall-to-wall carpeting so he never went hungry.

"I'z lookin' fo a frien'," said the bug. "The Oz get lonely sumtimez."

With that the boy and the bug started a friendship, with the boy spending a good deal of time sitting cross-legged on the floor chatting up the bug. The boy asked the bug about his siblings, his mother, his age, his favorite things and more.

The bug wanted to know what life outside the rec room was like, what snowflakes felt like and what the boy ate. The two never ran out of things to say to each other. They played together, and Mitchell brought cookie crumbs, bread crumbs and other tiny tidbits for his pal.

"I eats dust, spida webs, an' stuffs dat fall in da cahpet. Bug don' care. The Oz eat pretty much anyting, 'cept pins, wire, an' stuffs like dat."

Mitchell was an A student in school, but after a few weeks, his schoolwork suffered; he wasn't doing his assignments. The boy spent most of his time indoors, doing nothing but sitting on the floor talking to himself, his mother observed.

"Why don't you go outside and ride your bicycle? Play a computer game? Do your homework?" she asked.

After Mitchell begged off with "I don' wanna," his mother pressed him and he told her about his new friend, a bug that lives in their rug and talks to him. This is what prompted Mrs. Hally to take Mitchell to the family doctor, who listened to the absurd story.

"Lots of children have imaginary friends," the doctor said.

"Yes," the mother countered, "when they're four or five, not when they are nearly pre-teen."

"Oh, Mrs. Hally, he'll get over it." The doctor added, "Or perhaps he'll become a writer."

Mrs. Hally insisted the doctor to "do something" to get young Mitchell's mind off talking to insects and back on his schoolwork and reality. After inflicting a battery of tests on the kid all of which proved negative, the doctor referred the boy to a child psychiatrist at the urging of Mitchell's mother. She was certain her only child had a hidden brain tumor or a rare, neurological disease.

The specialist ran his own time-consuming and fruitless tests. Nothing! The boy's mother made a pest of herself, pushing the specialist to "do more." So, the shrink relented and prescribed an array of meds, notably antipsychotics and other nasty drugs for hallucinations, loss of contact with reality and other mental aberrations.

Side effects soon surfaced. Mitchell experienced dullness; he couldn't concentrate. He developed stomach aches, headaches, chills and a nasty rash, but he didn't tell anyone but Ozzie.

After that, his mother found Mitchell on the floor convulsing and called the EMT's. The boy nearly died. Mitchell was admitted to the hospital, and the family doctor rushed to his side.

"We're stopping all meds," said the doctor. "And we'll be keeping him overnight for observation."

Mitchell's mom went home, and in the morning she prepared to leave for the hospital. She hurriedly grabbed an open box of Cheerios and a paper cup for an on-the-run breakfast. Headed for the garage, Mrs. Hally rushed through the rec room and dropped the cereal on the rug.

"I have no time for this." she told herself. "I've got to go."

As she stopped reluctantly to scoop it up, she heard a tiny voice say,

"I'z Ozzie, what's yo name?"

Moral of the story: Clean your carpeting!

The Polish Princess

Word Count: 360
Reading Time: just under a minute 30 seconds

Malgorzata Czesgotski was an American of Polish descent who used the name Margaret because people could deal with it better than the Polish version. She was called Marge, Margie, Madge, Midge or Margo but in her heart she was always Malgorzata.

The woman loved her nationality, she loved the rich Polish culture, tradition, history, lovely Polish pottery, beautiful Polish amber, Chopin, and delicious Polish food but mostly Polish food.

Malgorzata learned to prepare kielbasa and kiszka, golabki, and pierogi. A fabulous baker, she excelled at baking goodies like chrusciki, kolaczki and babka, which she shared with her friends when she didn't gobble up all the goodies herself. She ate more than her share of Polish dills, pickled beets and pickled red cabbage.

One day, Dr. Coughlin Emfazema told her to stop eating salty Polish food because her blood pressure was sky high. "I'm Polish, I can't do that. Everything we eat is salty. I'll die if I can't have my pickled pig's feet."

"You'll die if you do," said the doctor, exiting the room and moving on to the next patient. Dr. Emfazema always seemed to be threatening patients with death.

Margaret/Margie/Madge/whoever went home and cried because there was nothing she could eat anymore.

The next day her friend, Agnieszka, brought over a basket of morel mushrooms she had just gathered. Aggie told her, "If you don't pick wild mushrooms, you can't call yourself Polish."

The sad Miss M looked at the morels, with their hollow, pitted hats. Then she tried the delectable mushrooms sautéed and became wild about them. Nothing she'd ever tasted were as yummy as these nutty-flavored morsels. Here was the food of royalty.

The Polish princess resumed being Polish again, learning the art of finding/preparing morels from her friend, Agnieszka. Malgorzata studied up on all the edible mushrooms in the forest. She soon became expert at selecting tasty fungi, except for the time when she was still learning, and took a tiny nibble of an Amanita mushroom the legendary Destroying Angel that kills your liver—and had to have her stomach pumped!

Oops!

Moral of the story: They say wild mushrooms are to die for!

Get Off The Road!

Word Count: 449
Reading Time: a minute 45 seconds

Carlotta Streeter was a lady of indeterminate age fighting for her independence.

Her son begged her to surrender her car keys after she was seen driving on the wrong side of the road. But Carlotta chose to keep driving until her '98 Cadillac gave up the ghost, or she couldn't get in and out of the car whichever came first. She was thinking another year.

Carlotta filled up with gas on her monthly trip to 7-11 and wouldn't you know it? Somebody yelled, "Get off the road!" just because she was doing 15 mph creeping home. She had been hearing that a lot lately.

The woman took driving precautions: She avoided night driving, rush hour traffic, the expressway, drunks, trucks, RV road hogs, road ragers and text-happy millennials.

But sometimes all Carlotta's efforts were not good enough. She cut down her driving to essentials. She didn't want her son coming around and causing trouble. She made an extra set of keys and hid them where he'd never look.

On April 15th, Carlotta took the Caddie out for a run to the post office, the last day to file taxes, definitely essential. It rained lightly when Carlotta left home but on the way back, there was a torrential downpour. Between her cataracts and fog, she could hardly see out the windshield. She kept making right turns to get where she wanted to go and took it extra slowly. Carlotta got lost cutting through the industrial section of town, and more than once hit the gas instead of the brake.

"Maybe next month, not next year," she thought.

Carlotta was skittish, especially when she noticed a cop car following closely behind that seemed to come out of nowhere. It was only a half-mile to home, so Carlotta tried to outrun him. She accelerated to a clip of 25 mph but couldn't shake him. The faster she drove, the more he hung on like a junkyard dog. As the heavens poured down, the cop started flashing his lights. Carlotta pressed on.

She reached the flooded underpass near her house. She didn't know how deep the water was, but she guessed the Caddie could take it. Guess again! Carlotta was stranded in her nearly-floating car. The cop, who was following only to warn her about the danger, came to her rescue.

"Maybe next week. No, definitely this week," she said out loud, as the cop pulled her out of the car, submerged wheel-high.

"How about right now?" chided the cop.

Shortly thereafter, Carlotta Streeter tore up her driver's license and gave it to her son as a birthday present. But she kept the spare key.

Moral of the story: Curse the millennials!

Alien

Word Count: 490
Reading Time: two minutes

Venus always dreamed of seeing a UFO. She lived in a remote part of upper Michigan where ghost stories and sightings of UFOs abounded, but she never thought she'd be caught up in the paranormal. Life in the woods was peaceful, and the only strange sights were raccoons in the dark peering in her windows.

The stargazer liked to go out looking at the night sky, gazing at the full moon or watching for an aurora borealis at the right time of year. Sometimes she saw something spectacular like a meteorite streaking across the sky, but never a UFO.

One clear night while driving home from church bingo, Venus glanced up and saw what she thought was a plane, though it made no sound. Venus took out her binoculars for a better look. She saw a strange, circular flat object with a panel of lights, like headlights, beaming down toward the ground. "What's that?" she asked herself, but she already knew.

Venus called her husband to tell him to look out the window. Fast asleep, her husband wasn't happy when she woke him. By the time he reluctantly got up, the object was gone.

As she drove home, Venus felt strange. Nothing was there, but she couldn't shake the creepy feeling of being watched. Venus turned the corner of the block where she lived and spotted the object again. Now it was closer, much closer, barely skimming the treetops. She plainly saw it was a UFO.

The curious woman picked up her binoculars and spied aliens inside at the controls, aliens with big, bald, green heads, green faces and seemingly menacing expressions. Sure, Venus wished to see a flying saucer some night, but now that the night was here, not so much!

The spacecraft circled the block, and the occupants were aware of her presence. She called the police, but the call failed. Venus tried again. Her cell phone went dead.

Venus didn't want to bring aliens home with her so she sped away. Halfway down the street, she noticed the UFO following her. Venus drove at breakneck speed, and the UFO took chase. She headed for a nearby, heavily wooded area hoping to throw the UFO off her trail. In the woods, her engine stalled. Venus panicked.

"I don't want to be abducted by aliens," she whimpered. "They're coming to get me!"

The frightened woman abandoned her car and hid in the underbrush a quarter mile away, until she felt the coast was clear. After about an hour, Venus returned to her car and drove home watching tentatively for the UFO. It was gone. Venus pulled into the garage, closed the overhead door and heaved a sigh of relief.

From a corner of the garage, a squeaky voice said, "Do you have a cup of coffee? I come in peace."

Venus fainted.

Moral of the story: Always keep a pot of coffee on, in case visitors drop in.

Snoopy

Word Count: 213
Reading Time: just over 45 seconds

Little Melinda was a mischievous eighth-grader who thought she could pull a fast one. Every Christmas she raided the hiding place where her mother stashed the wrapped holiday gifts.

When no one was looking, little Melinda rattled, squeezed and shook them to guess what goodies waited within the colorful boxes. The little snoop very carefully unwrapped each one to see if she guessed right. Then she'd very carefully rewrap each gift so nobody was the wiser.

Melinda was so good at her devilish deed that it was difficult to tell that somebody tampered with the packages. This made her squeal with delight, knowing she knew something she shouldn't know, and nobody else knew she knew. Melinda did this for several years and got away with it. She thought she could go on fooling everybody as long as it amused her.

Last Christmas Melinda got her comeuppance. The little girl rifled through all the loot when she noticed the prettiest package of all. How had she missed it? She opened it quickly, but not fast enough.

Three rat traps sprang on her fingers. She let out a painful, "M-O-T-H-E-R!!!" that was heard by everyone in the house. Busted! Snoopy's number was up.

Moral of the story: Get to the gifts before they are wrapped.

Saving Mr. Junkett

Word Count: 460
Reading Time: just over a minute 45 seconds

As a child, Mr. Junkett amassed marbles, stickers, comic books, baseball cards and all the rest of the things boys enjoy.

When the kid was 18, his mother told him to toss out or, at least, put all of his childhood playthings in the old toy chest for storage. But the teenager just let his things be. She harped without success.

After mom slipped and sprained her ankle on marbles that rolled out of his room, the kid came home from school and found that his room had been violated. The boy's mother had either thrown out or given to Goodwill every vestige of his childhood.

That's why the grown man collected things; not for knowledge and learning, not for acquisition of wealth but for ages-old outrage about loss of privacy and possessions.

At first Mr. Junkett just kept old photos, postcards and souvenirs, such as matchbook covers, of places he'd visited. He went on to collect frig magnets, canceled stamps and pennies, nothing of any worth. After amassing a six-foot high pile of *Racing Forms* by his easy chair, Mr. Junkett gathered coffee cups with decals of scantily-clad gals.

Next, Mr. Junkett turned the page on normalcy by filling glass jars with toe nail clippings, belly button fluff and earwax. He had a hard time parting with rotting food. Fruit flies in the kitchen made it resemble a snowstorm. Mr. Junkett had a hard time throwing anything out. It was difficult to climb out of a room. His home looked like a loathsome hovel. Things surpassed healthy collecting and entered the realm of hoarding.

As Mr. Junkett became something of a wampus, his relatives organized an intervention and told him to get rid of his junk, or they would do it for him. The city threatened eviction. Thoughts of mom and her insensitivity came back to him. He stubbornly resisted any attempt to change. When he came home from work, the place was cleaned. It took 10 trips to the dump to save Mr. Junkett.

After that, Mr. Junkett was a broken man, until the day when he took a shovel and stopped at the corner of 5th and Main. There he dug up a street sign that said, "Children at Play." He carried off the sign and returned home pausing only at a display of fruit outside a produce market. He poached a couple of oranges and a banana and was gone.

Thus, Mr. Junkett replaced his old bad ways and took the first step toward a new direction in his life: big box stores, supermarkets, restaurants, drugstores, the choices were endless. He had hit upon a new hobby that would carry him through the rest of his life: shoplifting!

Moral of the story: Mothers are bullies.

Bugged

Word Count: 358
Reading Time: just under a minute 30 seconds

Citronella Von Trapp had entomophobia. Her fear of bugs started in childhood when the family lived in an inner city basement apartment that had a drain trap in the floor. The trap backed up when the street flooded with rain water.

If the little girl got up in the middle of the night to go potty, she'd find her bare feet in sewer water with floating feces. Quite often, she stepped on a cockroach fleeing for a lifeboat. Crunch! Those experiences left Citronella scarred for life.

When the phobic woman moved to Texas for work, Nella never realized it was primo bug paradise. The first time she saw a scorpion crawling on her bed covers with that predatory look about its pedipalps, was the last time Citronella Von Trapp lived in Texas. Bed bugs without borders hitchhiked with her when Nella moved to Minneapolis where the cold kills off most bugs, except bed bugs. She had Texan bed bugs she didn't know she had. Nella thought the bites on her neck were hickeys.

It should have been a bed bug tip-off when Nella spotted belongings stuffed in big, black garbage bags outside her neighbor's apartment and men from Orkin scurrying around the complex.

Nella's life was a horror story of woman versus bug. It got so bad she wouldn't eat dates because they looked like dried cockroaches. She was a nervous wreck trying to cope with anything that was small, black and moved. She was so paranoid with the annoying critters of daily life, she imagined spiders on her walls, cigarette beetles in her flour, centipedes and silverfish in her bath tub, not to mention the nasty bed bugs that really were there, robbing her of sleep and tormenting her dreams.

Nella was about ready to check into the funny farm when everything changed. Dropping by a neighborhood bar to knock back a few and drown her sorrows, she met the man of her dreams, the guy she had been waiting for all her life.

Citronella met Bugsy, the exterminator, they married and lived happily ever after!

Moral of the story: There's someone out there for everyone.

Phony Baloney

Word Count: 339
Reading Time: just over a minute 15 seconds

Caz Bowers, a/k/a Kazimierz Bowkowski, was a successful lawyer, ashamed of his Old World background. His father, still in Poland, sent him to live with relatives in Chicago's Logan Square after his mother died, in hope that his son would live his American dream.

The boy worked his way through college at Northwestern, won a scholarship to Harvard Law School and made his father smile.

He moved to New York, where he landed a job with a huge law firm, but not before changing his legal name to Caz Bowers, because his Polish name embarrassed him. In time Caz worked his way up to senior partner.

Caz' father remained in Poland with his daughter, where father and daughter worked in an uncle's shoe repair shop in small town Kazimierz Dolny. When their father died, Caz' sister, Kasia, wrote her brother and asked him to take her in, now that she was all alone.

When Kasia Bowkowski arrived, the differences between the polished New York lawyer and his unsophisticated sister who spoke halting English became apparent and caused a snag to Caz in the social circle in which he moved.

Caz tried to keep Kasia tucked away in his expansive Central

Park West high rise where no one would see her, and no one would discover his secret.

The pretentious New York lawyer suffered through many near-slips, as Kasia refused to be confined to a shut-away situation, no matter how luxurious.

Kasia loved to roam the neighborhood and make casual friends at a nearby Starbucks. She was proud to be Polish and rightly so.

His sister didn't have to stomach Caz' affected airs any longer when she met a rich Wall Street stockbroker over coffee who loved her charming accent and winning ways and didn't give a hoot about anything else. She was his fair lady.

The girl married Wainwright Carouthers III, bought the Central Park building where Caz lived and swiftly gave her phony baloney brother an eviction notice.

Quizlet? Where's the nearest Starbucks to Central Park West?

Bird Brain

Word Count: 166
Reading Time: just under 45 seconds

Phoebe was an avid birdwatcher who entertained herself by observing birds from the window of her fourth floor apartment. She peered down into the trees and spotted the birds feeding their nestlings and teaching them to fly.

One day, Phoebe bought a bird book that had a unique feature: bird sounds which mimicked the calls of all her feathered friends. She had a field day with the book and often sat at her window projecting the sounds outdoors.

Birds flew past her window frantically looking for the source of the calls. It confused them and interfered with finding mates. It delighted bird brain to trick the birds into thinking the sounds were real. The birds, however, were not equally amused and let her know.

Phoebe took to her window the next morning but couldn't see a thing. It was covered from side to side and top to bottom with bird dud, obliterating her view.

Quizlet: Who has the higher IQ: A whip-poor-will or a Phoebe?

Express Yourself!

Word Count: 521
Reading Time: just over two minutes

A non-artist named Julie Chicago dreamed of becoming a Renoir, a Rembrandt or a Raphael.

As a child, little Julie liked to draw and paint. After she decorated the family's home with permanent Magic Marked walls, her mother removed all markers, pens, crayons, colored pencils, paint and brushes from their home.

In the first grade at Chicago's school, tests were administered to determine the children's artistic talent. Julie's results came back: forget about it. And her, a possible grandsomething, second cousin once remove or other sketchy relative of famed Windy City artist, Judy "The Dinner Party" Chicago. Shameful! Impossible!

A special teacher, Miss Moroccomich, came to Judy's school for fifth grade art classes. After the child made fun of the teacher's name, she was punished by exclusion from the class. That just made her want art so much more.

In college, the girl major in art. She immersed herself in art history and gloried in Ancient times, the Renaissance, Surrealism. Julie could tell you the life story of every artist from Nicholas of Verdun through Durer, Titian, El Greco, Gainsborough, Goya, and Gauguin to Klee, Rauschenberg and Stella.

Julie Chicago visited museums on the weekend when she wasn't working at her ho-hum job as a grocery checker. If there was a workshop or a lecture on Humanism, Julie would rendezvous there with friends. She covered art in all its forms, but there was something missing: Julie had no artistic talent, none. The long ago tests were right.

She couldn't even draw a straight line. Julie had trouble with color by numbers; she couldn't stay inside the lines in an adult coloring book.

One day, Julie met Joyce Giotto, a fabulous artist who could draw, paint, decorate and do just about everything artistic. The no-talent art aficionado couldn't wait to take in one of Joyce's workshops. She studied under Joyce for a few weeks, but Julie's oils, acrylics, and watercolors were pathetic. Julie could barely hold a brush and yet, she aspired to be LIKE Joyce if not BE Joyce.

But Julie's clever art teacher knew how to bring out the artist in Julie that both of them knew was hiding somewhere inside her, just waiting to express itself.

The next workshop Joyce Giotto held was Abstract Expressionism. The teacher extolled the genius of de Kooning and Rothko and gave Julie Chicago a huge canvas on which to work.

Julie was overwhelmed. She didn't know what to do with it, so in desperation she started throwing strings dipped in paint at the canvas. Releasing all her inhibitions, Julie realized it was fun.

"I've just had a brainstorm," Julie said, encouraged by her first attempt.

She grabbed another life-sized canvas and a giant-sized squirt bottle of mustard and splattered it all over the blank canvas. Then she did it again with a squirt bottle of chocolate syrup.

"It's practical," Julie Chicago told herself, "it's lickable." This piece tickled her taste for art.

The teacher came running in, looked over Julie's work and declared, "Behold! The next Jackson Pollock!"

Moral of the story: If you have a taste for art, check your pantry.

House Dust Hezzie

Word Count: 294
Reading Time: just under a minute 15 seconds

House dust Hezzie was comfortable with the status quo. For her, house cleaning was a dirty word. Her feather duster had spider webs on it; her vacuum cleaner hadn't been used since the '90s.

Booger, Hezzie's black cat, (or was it grey?) slept in the cozy, dust bunnies beneath her bed with the mites. When Hezzie turned on the ceiling fan, it snowed; when she walked across her tile floor, she made footprints; dust furrows tracked in the rug. But the problem went further than dust.

It was a bother for Hezzie to use her dishwasher, so she piled dirty dishes in the kitchen sink. When she ran out, she used paper plates. She'd wait to recycle until the *Enquirer* stack in her living room got so high and unsteady, it toppled and buried Booger, who then used it as kitty litter. Hez didn't need the washer/drying in her apartment because she never washed clothes. It was easier to wear the same clothes over and over. She painted her fingernails so she didn't have to clean them. Since she seldom left her apartment, so what?

Hezzie stayed clear of the apartment manager, a former military man and obvious neat freak. Every time Rutger Goebbels saw her, he threatened her to clean up her act. But the Hez was not disposed to overhauling her happy home.

One day, while she watched marathon TV, the garbage got too ripe. A neighbor noticed a rank odor emanating from house dust heaven. He thought someone died. He thought it might be Hezzie. He called the apartment manager."Enough!" said Rutger.

That was the day Hezzie's happy home wasn't happy anymore. Hezzie got the heave-ho.

Moral of the story: Take out the garbage before someone gets wind of you.

Hypochondriac

Word Count: 322
Reading Time: just over a minute 15 seconds

Placebo Domingo was the last of 12 children. His father worked three jobs to provide for the family and was never home. The little boy's mother was committed to a mental institution shortly after Placebo entered kindergarten.

Older siblings reared the boy, but not well. He more or less raised himself. As a result, the little guy realized that only when he got measles, mumps or chickenpox did anyone give a rap about him. It was no surprise that Placebo grew to manhood supporting the emotional baggage of his childhood.

His doctor examined him and pronounced him fit, but being in good health was bad news for a hypochondriac like Placebo. His future was uncertain. No more attention. Placebo started inventing ailments. Every other week he took a new worry to the doctor. If he coughed, he was sure it was TB. The doctor ran tests. No TB.

If his heart skipped a beat, congenital heart failure. Tests negative.

If his ankles swelled, renal failure. More tests, no kidney problems.

Headaches: brain tumor. No such luck.

He called 911 many times and went by ambulance to the ER.

He liked going in style and the EMT's showed him respect. This went on for several years until 911 told him to drive himself to the hospital.

His doctor canceled appointments with him instead of the other way around. When Placebo called, the nurses told him he reached the wrong number. Placebo cried wolf so much that the medical staff no longer listened. Placebo was just too healthy to get sick.

Then an awful thing happened. His health insurance carrier, groaning under the weight of all his doctor bills, tests and ambulance charges over the last few years, pulled the plug and canceled his insurance.

Interestingly, when Placebo had to fork over the money from his own pocket, his hypochondria suddenly disappeared.

Moral of the story: If you crave attention, buy a dog!

The Lottery

Word Count: 449
Reading Time: just over a minute 45 seconds

Jackhammer Jake Buckleberry worked for the Department of Public Works. His job was maintaining streets, storm drains and sewer lines.

JJ used a 75-pound jackhammer to tear up streets and patch them up again. He was a big, strong guy who carried a lunch box, wore a red-checkered shirt and loved to stop after work for a beer with the guys.

You wouldn't peg Jackhammer Jake for a cerebral type who dabbled in fortune-telling. But after a chunk of concrete flew up and hit him in the head, the man began to "see" things he never saw before.

While flipping channels on his TV one night, Jake came across a weekly broadcast of winning lottery numbers. Just for fun, before the next numbers were drawn, he guessed the Pick Three, all correct and in sequence. He did this for a couple of weeks with perfect accuracy, then graduated to Pick Four and finally to Power Ball. He was never wrong.

Jake mentioned it to the guys at work, and they asked for the numbers so they could buy lottery tickets. He was reluctant to give out any information. He felt he would lose his powers or worse unless the money went to charity.

After he made his buddies promise to give 50 per cent to charity, he gave them the winning numbers for the next week's lottery. Soon his co-workers were raking in dough hand over fist. Jake stopped helping them when the nagging thoughts came back. It didn't feel right.

His wife, Whinona, wanted to know why he couldn't buy lottery tickets to benefit his own family.

"Every day I wash other peoples' dirty laundry and clean their toilets. With just one big win, I could stop working and stay home with the kids," she whined.

But Jake wouldn't do it. He couldn't betray his powers. He could only help others in need, not himself or his family.

"Jake," said his wife, "our kids are growing out of their clothes faster than I can get to Goodwill to get more."

Whinona kept working on him. Then she pulled the wife card. "If you loved me, you'd buy me a lottery ticket." She went on, "Think of me as a charity. I'm sick of being poor. Just one, honey, and I promise I'll never ask again."

That did it! Whinona finally wore down Jake's defenses. He bought a Power Ball ticket, just one, for Whinona. Jake still had misgivings that this action would bring him bad luck. And it did.

Jackhammer Jake won big, and the next day at work, he stumbled on broken pavement and fell head first into an open manhole. They never found him.

Quizlet: "Sewerly" you jest?

Nature Girl

Word Count: 554
Reading Time: two minutes 15 seconds

Beverly Bumstead loved the outdoors. She worshipped summer and spent most days hanging out at the city park walking her Jack Russell terrier, Killer. The blonde cutie was interested in anything and everything connected with nature.

She recently met a lady from England at the park. It turned out Hermione Higginbotham lived on Beverly's block. Bev was curious about a fun hobby of Hermione's that involved gathering wildlings from the woods and making her own tasty tea with the leaves.

Practically overnight, they began a friendship when Hermione invited Beverly to her home for tea and homemade scones. Hermione treated Bev to three British demitasse cups of tea, each delicate cup with a different, fragrant and delectable taste.

Hermione explained how she picked, washed, dried, pulverized and inserted the leaves into fillable paper tea bags she bought at the supermarket. For the finishing touch, Hermione secured each little tea bag with a pretty pink ribbon and carefully tucked the bags into an ornate wooden tea box Hermione found while shopping at Piccadilly Circus.

Nature girl decided that day she too would take up Hermione's unique tea hobby. Hermione gifted Bev with a dozen empty bags to launch her hobby and made a date when the two could go for a stroll, so she could teach Bev all about selecting leaves.

But Bev was impatient and couldn't wait a single day.

The thicket started where her backyard ended, so Bev and Killer took a walk in the woods. Bev hunted for plants like the ones Hermione made into tea. They all looked alike to someone like Bev who wasn't savvy to forest vegetation.

Killer scampered ahead, and when Bev caught up with him, he was rolling around in a patch of beautiful green foliage. The leaves looked shiny and attractive when the sun peaked through the trees and illuminated them. Bev bent down to smell the plants. A leaf tickled her nose.

Bev thought that the leaves looked sort of like Hermione's tea leaves, and anything so pretty and shiny should be great. Even if they didn't have a discernible perfume, the plants had cute, yellowish-green flowers. That seemed reasonable so Bev pulled out a bunch of Killer's plastic doo doo bags from her pocket. As Bev gathered leaves, her terrier luxuriated in his verdant playground.

"I can't wait to surprise Hermione," Bev told Killer.

Once home, the new tea recruit rinsed and set her treasured bounty on the kitchen counter. The leaves needed a lot of space to air dry. They took over the kitchen counter, the dining room table and a hutch. Two days later the leaves were dried and ready for the next step, which was a relief, because Killer was jumping up and spreading them all over the house.

After that, Killer started barking, biting his feet and feverishly trying to scratch his butt. Bev's hands started itching and swelling, and before long a red, nasty rash popped up on her nose and all over her hands.

Hermione happened by about the time blisters appeared on Beverly's skin. All Hermione could say was, "Oh, no!" as she loaded Beverly and Killer into her SUV and took them to the emergency room.

Poison ivy tea, anyone?

Moral of the story: If you want an outdoor hobby, try sunbathing.

The Trip To Nowhere

Word Count: 425
Reading Time: a minute 45 seconds

With a name like Robin Springsted, one would think this curious Midwesterner would become a meteorologist. But that was not to be.

Robin became a downhill skiing instructor indulging in nature-oriented hobbies including waterfall rappelling, water witching and collecting bugs. There was one hobby that she especially relished, but she had an opportunity to pursue it only once a year.

Those who live in Northern Wisconsin endure a long, cold winter and look forward to spring with gusto. So it was with the anticipation of a child at Christmas that Robin set out on her yearly motor trek to find spring heading south as the geese flew north.

Timing was perfect, too, because Robin was unemployed in spring (summer and fall too.) She supplemented her income in the off-seasons by wading in water traps and retrieving errant balls at the golf course which paid for her trip to nowhere. It was her annual fly-by-the-seat-of-your pants trip, and Robin loved it. She never knew where her trip would take her, but she always knew when she got there.

As a member of the local phenology club, Robin learned that spring cannot be officially declared until the six signs of phenological spring exist. She had seen lake ice break up—first sign!

She already saw migratory birds, check that one off the list. Once in her car, a dead skunk signaled road kill, the third sign. If insects hit her windshield, it was sign number four. With two signs to go and just over the state line in Illinois, spring seemed imminent.

In Peoria she saw dandelions in bloom, but Robin had to drive to Cairo to find the sixth and final sign of spring: half-open leaves on trees.

Now Robin knew exactly where spring in the Midwest had officially arrived. To figure out how long it took to get from place to place, she calculated the miles between home and the city of spring, and divided by 16, the number of miles spring travels north each day (or approximately 100 miles a week.)

Robin returned home just in time to greet spring and tell everyone when spring would officially arrive in their town. Since many of them were already looking at bedding plants, they weren't impressed.

She also returned home to discover that while she was gone, a tree had fallen on her house in a storm.

With her picture window shattered, a family of raccoons had taken up residence in her living room. Happy Spring!

Quizlet: What's a good place to buy bedding plants?

Cheap John's Wife

Word Count: 432
Reading Time: a minute 45 seconds

Cheap John's wife had the patience of a saint. She put up with her husband's bizarre ways for the three years they were married and never brought up the fact that they had nothing permanent, nothing of value; they lived in mean estate.

Their home was a run-down place on the edge of town. Somebody he knew let them live there rent free. The childless couple used a blow-up bed, folding chairs and orange crates for furniture.

The Cheap Johns had no dishes or silverware. They used disposables and washed them for re-use. Instead of ovenware, Cheap John folded the edges of aluminum foil and made makeshift pans. He bought dented cans and expired food at supermarkets. No need for a pantry, they kept just enough edibles to last a few days.

Most young women Mrs. CJ's age like clothes, shoes and makeup. Cheap John bought his wife rummage sale leftovers and Barbie doll lipstick that he picked up from the clearance bin at the Dollar Store, as well as tiny tubes of toothpaste, packets of aspirin and other bathroom supplies. Mrs. Cheap John used them and said nothing. Her husband boiled down broken pieces of bar soap and made fresh bars. The Mrs. never questioned what Cheap John did.

This was the only life 21-year-old Mrs. Cheap John had ever known, since she came from abject poverty.

They acquired no books, no files and no photos. Cheap John resisted any attempt to have his picture taken. He kept a low profile by staying off the internet and using a disposable phone. He wanted things that way, and she went along with it.

Cheap John and his wife spent their time playing cards and watching TV on a little portable screen. He pulled the shades, and at 9 p.m. sharp, sooner in winter, he put out the lights. The couple kept to themselves and didn't participate in social activities. Even their relatives thought they were dead.

Then one night everything changed. Cheap John went out for a walk and was the victim of a drive-by shooting. It turned out that he was not only cheap but in Witness Protection.

Three months after Cheap John died, his young widow met and married an improvident billionaire who treated her like a princess.

The former Mrs. Cheap John stomped on her miserable tube of doll lipstick and ordered boxes of Chanel makeup and designer clothes imported from Paris, as she became Mrs. Regis Pierpont III, and lived the rest of her life enveloped in luxury.

Quizlet: Where do you go to meet a billionaire?

The F Word

Word Count: 382
Reading Time: a minute 30 seconds

Marion "Bibi" Ostermeister was a librarian with an allied hobby. She had a thing for words.

As a precocious child, Marion learned to read at an early age and consumed the dictionary like other kids read Dr. Seuss.

As she got older, Bibi started a collection, not of stamps, or dolls but of words, glorious words, homonyms with at least four or more definitions like rest or lie; glamorous words like flesh or fish that sounded swishy when pronounced slowly; palindromes (racecar, kayak, mom.) Bibi also collected alliteration: "Peter Piper picked;" assonances including penitence and reticence; words with six or more syllables, like responsibility.

When she found words with nine or more syllables like socioeconomically or individualistically, she was overjoyed. It didn't take much to entertain Bibi.

At 21 she had an affair with Roget. She found 2,984 synonyms for the word "drunk," the most for any word. How proud Bibi was to unearth this vital fact everyone would want to know at cocktail parties! She figured she could pick up guys at bars by relating facts about words that she found captivating.

"Hi, sailor, did you know that the fear of peanut butter sticking to the roof of your mouth is called arachibutyrophobia? Or the medical term for stomach growling is borborygmus?" What fun for Bibi! And one reason why she never had a boyfriend and probably never will.

"More English words start with S than any other letter," she blathered. "There are 293 pages of S words, or 29,762 S words in the dictionary, followed fairly closely by 25,647 C words and F words only number 11,588," announced Bibi to unimpressed patrons.

Marion the librarian spent more and more time playing with words than doing her work. One day when she should have been shelving novels, checking out books for patrons, and helping old people with computer literacy and those without tech skills, she found the longest word in the English language: pneumonoultramicroscopicsilicovolcanoconiosis.

While Bibi was busy counting the number of letters in it, the head librarian approached her and said: M A R I O N! Here's a F word for your collection: F I R E D. You are F I R E D!

Moral of the story: What's a 10-letter word that means out of work?

GOING UP?

Word Count: 771
Reading Time: just over three minutes

Ninotchka Yuodsnukis was a tired, old European cleaning lady who worked past her prime at Chicago's Willis Tower, formerly Sears Tower.

She married Zakric, who survived the seiche of '54, the 10-foot high, inland tidal wave that swept his father out to a watery grave in Lake Michigan. On that fateful summer day so long ago when the seiche hit, 12-year old Zakric and his papa were fishing on the breakwater at Montrose Harbor.

Over the years Zakric held many noteworthy jobs, one of which was as a stock handler at the old Union Stock Yards which closed 40 years ago. Zakric, who had COPD, was a hard worker but he didn't follow doctor's orders to move away from the Windy City for his health. Zak couldn't give up his fondness for Ben's Shrimp, Chicago hot dogs or Wrigley Field, so he died.

Ninotchka was left to clean the Tower offices and go home to an empty apartment in Bucktown.

Since Zak's passing, Nina worked her way up at the Tower and eventually became the head cleaning lady for floors 98 to 108. She did her job, and she did it well. Ninotchka was proud of her accomplishment, as so she should be, even as her job became more of a struggle every day. She often left work ready to drop.

When a cleaning lady gets arthritic flat feet and needs a bottle of Advil to get through the week, it's time to turn in the pail and mop for good. Ninotchka promised her children she'd retire the day the Cubs won the World Series. It was her little joke until the Cubs actually pulled it off.

Nina hoped to hold off retiring until she was 75, but suddenly decided she would turn in her notice the following Monday. Her body was giving out, and she was ready.

When Mrs. Y came to work that night, the doorman mentioned that there was an elevator problem on several of the floors in her stack of the huge building complex, but that it would be fixed by quitting time.

Her shift ended at two a.m. and Nina was relieved.

"Thank God it's Friday," she said to herself.

Her feet were killing her, and all she wanted to do was go home and soak them. Nina limped into the elevator. Then it stalled.

"I can't hike down 108 floors."

The tired, old lady repeatedly pressed the elevator's floor buttons.

This was not to be Ninotchka Yuodsnukis' lucky day.

The elevator inched down to 94. Nothing happened. She picked up the emergency telephone.

"Hello? Hello?"

A low, scary voice at the other end said, "going down?" and began cackling hideously.

The doors opened on 94 and a man in a clown suit uttered a demonic scream and lunged at her. Just as he charged the elevator, the doors shut in his face. Nina shook with fear.

The elevator then took on a life of its own, opening to a floor where a pile of luggage sat—the baggage of Ninotchka's life. She reflected on the baggage she's carried. The old woman's life flashed before her. After that, the elevator zoomed down to the building's basement so fast Nina nearly fell down.

When the doors opened, this wasn't any lower level Mrs.Y had ever seen.

"I must be losing my mind."

The cleaning lady saw a horrific sight: the floor flooded with oozing, viscid globs in an odious cesspool of filth. A decomposing reliquiae of cadavers floated on the surface, bobbing like apples in the murky brew. Outstretched arms flailing madly in grisly agony rose from the stomach-churning cesspool.

The elevator moved up to the main floor. It stopped, but the doors didn't open. Nina panicked.

"Get me out of here!" she yelled, kicking and banging on the elevator door. There was an interminably long wait and nothing happened. Ninotchka started to fade.

"Please, God, help me. I'm tired. I want to go home."

Slowly, there was a gradual assent, as the elevator crept back to the top of the building.

But the elevator didn't stop. It kept going! The elevator went through the roof.

A beautiful, bright white light greeted the lady as the elevator soared high above the building. The doors opened. She saw Zak smiling at her. The light got brighter and brighter until Ninotchka Yuodsnukis went to the Light.

In the morning, they found the cleaning lady lying on the floor of the elevator, her head rested on a soft mop head, her body cradled in a fetal position, a calm smile on her face.

Moral of the story: Avoid elevators.

Blarney

Word Count: 558
Reading Time: two minutes 15 seconds

Nelly became Kelly on St. Patrick's Day.

Through a gross error on her mother's part, Nelly came into the world the day before St. Pat's Day. Why her mother couldn't have waited to deliver, Nelly had no clue, but the snafu was a lifelong disappointment to her.

The English miss wanted to be born on a festive holiday, marked by parades, wearing funny clothes and drinking green beer. March 16th had none of that.

Nelly remedied it by celebrating her birthday on St. Patrick's Day and calling herself Kelly. Only Social Security and the IRS knew her real birthday and a few relatives who were sworn to secrecy under pain of mortal sin. It got so she believed the fabrication, and all went well for Kelly.

Last year, the little minx decided to go a step further so she could tell all her friends she went to Ireland for her St. Patrick's Day birthday and kissed the Blarney Stone.

Kelly purportedly booked a flight out of Chicago on Aer Lingus and planned a memorable trip to the Emerald Isle, birthplace of Oscar Wilde and home of Tullamore Dew.

In fact, the Irish Whiskey Trail, with a stop at the new Tullamore Distillery, and a tour of Jameson's in Dublin were on her avowed agenda. Kelly also hoped to see the Guinness brewery, hoist the black stuff and visit the headquarters of the Guinness Book of World Records at the same time.

So many places to go and see Ireland: The iconic Cliffs of Moher (Galway Bay), the jaw-dropping Ring of Kerry, the moon-like Burren and Moneygall, the home of Barack Obama.

"What?" Kelly doubted, reading a brochure: "The tiny village of Moneygall flaunts itself as the home of the 44th President of the United States? Blarney! Tell HIM that." She learned Obama's great great great grandfather on his mother's side lived in Moneygall during the Irish Potato Famine before immigrating to the US. The only time Obama ever visited Moneygall was on St. Patrick's Day, 2011. But the Moneygallians are sticking to their story. Kelly laughed.

The highlight of Kelly's trip was definitely a drive to Castle Blarney to kiss the Blarney Stone, said to bestow the gift of gab on kissers.

As test of her physical fitness, Kelly supposedly climbed the 128 steps to the highest point of the castle through a narrow, dungeon-like passageway. She peered down into the 300-foot crevasse that separated her from the Blarney Stone on the opposite side of a rock wall.

Instructions were to sit down, lean backwards over the edge into the crevasse, put both arms over her head and grab bars on the other side of the formidable hole. She dangled over the edge of the abyss, as attendants held her to prevent Kelly from falling. She was glad she hadn't come before the grab bars were installed to prevent risking life and limb.

"And they charge money for this?" Kelly asked herself.

Kelly suffered a bout of acrophobia from the dizzying height and hurt her back leaning over to kiss the Blarney Stone. She's been wearing a back brace, but all the more exciting blarney to tell her friends once she got home, especially since Nelly never even went to Ireland.

Moral of the story: If you're lucky enough to pretend to be Irish, you're lucky enough.

Lady In The Snow

Word Count: 543
Reading Time: just under two minutes 15 seconds

Kristofer Noel was driving to church in a ferocious blizzard. Visibility was dangerously poor, and the temperature had plunged to 10 below zero, with conditions deteriorating by the minute.

The man had just come from the hospital where his wife, stricken with severe pneumonia, was fighting for her life. He was trying to make it to Midnight Mass to pray for her.

He had trouble keeping his car on the unplowed road. Suddenly, his headlights beamed on a figure standing on the side of the road. She was a slender, young woman in a long, white, robe-like dress wearing sandals and holding a newborn swaddled in a blanket.

Kris couldn't believe his eyes: a coatless woman with an infant in freezing cold, out in the middle of the night on Christmas?

He stopped the car abruptly and jumped out to help the woman.

"Wherever you're headed, let me give you a lift! You shouldn't be out in this snowstorm," he said. "Please," and he motioned toward the front seat of his car.

"Are you going my way?" the woman asked.

"I'm headed to church," said Kristofer, "to pray for my wife who's in the hospital."

"I'm going there too," the lady replied.

He eased her and the baby into the car, then went around to the trunk and pulled out a pair of women's boots and two blankets.

"Have to be prepared for this weather!" he said, "My wife keeps a spare pair in the car for emergencies. Put them on."

"Thank you," said his passenger, "but I won't be needing them or the blankets."

Once he was back at the wheel, Kristofer noticed that the whole car had heated up; it was so hot that he turned off the heater and removed his windbreaker. The woman and child were radiating warmth.

Kristofer felt odd and couldn't bring himself to say a word.

He watched the road open up and the blizzard stop. He spotted the church steeple a mile away; they arrived at church in seconds. Kristofer let off the lady and baby at the front door, but not before she handed him a long-stemmed white rose that looked like it had just been plucked.

Kris put the rose in the car and all he could say was, "wait for me," as he drove off to the parking lot. He returned and asked Scully, the usher, where the young, coatless woman with the newborn was seated.

"You been drinkin?" It's 10 below out there. Nobody like that came in," Scully said.

Kristofer asked Fr. Hogan who was standing at the rear of church preparing for the start of Mass.

"Son, you must be mistaken," the priest replied.

Even Ben, the old guy, who always sat in the last pew and observed everyone coming and going, shook his head, "no."

After the stymied man searched the church and turned up nothing, he chose his pew and had one of the most extraordinarily-peaceful and spiritually-enriching moments of his life. It was then that Kristofer Noel knew in his heart that his wife would be alright.

When he returned to his ice-covered car after Mass, Kristofer noticed the white, dewy rose laying on the seat.

Moral of the story: Hitchhiking is against the law.

THE DREAMER

Word Count: 771
Reading Time: just over three minutes

Since early adulthood Michael Somnolenti was a prolific dreamer whose night time percolated with extravagant images. He anticipated sleeping as an adventure with lively, spirited happy goings-on.

One night, Michael had a dream like no other had ever been or would be again. The snoozer was seized by sudden, sharp, stabbing tortuous pain, as if being in the paralyzing jaws of a man-eating vise crushing his chest. Once the pain dissipated, Michael found himself sucked into a cold, foggy tunnel. Dark and damp inside, the space was similar to that of an immense vacuum cleaner powered by an invisible overwhelming force from which there was no pulling away.

Michael sensed the presence of others around him but the feeling was more frightening than reassuring. He was aware of a woman's perfume, the gamey scent of dirty underwear and a whiff of formaldehyde. The harder Michael fought the force of the tunnel, the more it overpowered him. Before long his spirit gave way to acceptance and he simply stopped fighting, allowing himself to be dipped, spun and lifted like the swirl on top a soft-serve ice cream cone.

The tunnel became a train, transporting Michael and the others to their final destination. The train stopped, the exit doors opened and all filed out anxious to proceed. At the end of the loading platform stood a conductor punching commuter tickets and putting stubs into the pink, satin-lined pockets of his snowy-white conductor's uniform.

As each passenger approached, the conductor said, "Straight ahead, to the left, to the right or lower level please." He motioned Michael toward a waiting area which appeared to be a motel room. Michael stood in front of the door waiting for guidance. The conductor said, "Don't you have the foggiest notion in hell where you're headed? Go in! And don't come back here."

Alarmed and confused, Michael entered the room. It appeared to be just another cheap motel room that a traveler gets stuck with when all the good places are gone.

The walls of the room were cinder block painted beige, with an orange frieze chair and an old, orange-and-brown striped tattered bedspread on the lumpy-looking twin bed. A wall clock above the bed had no hands on it and a TV on a rickety nightstand didn't work. A spot loomed on the thin, worn carpeting on which a dog had recently taken a dump.

Michael opened the ugly blood-stained drapes, but the conductor, the platform and the train were gone. He found a total void, a barren plain, a moonscape where the wind started up and built to tornadic level. Michael quickly pulled the drapes closed and rushed to exit the room, but the door was gone. He moved toward the nightstand looking for the comfort of the *Bible*, but there was none.

He entered the bathroom, where a sink had faucets that didn't turn and a toilet with only a seat suspended in air and no bowl beneath it; the seat clacked open and shut like a rattling set of false teeth. A leaky shower, with mold bleeding onto the grout between the wall tiles, dripped inky-black sludge out of the shower head with no way to turn it off and no place for it to go. The disgusting liquid filled the shower and began flooding the bathroom. Before long the filthy fluid consumed the entire motel room, and Michael feared he'd be swept away in the tide.

In this defining moment, Michael caught sight of something on the wall which effected calm resignation. It was something mounted in a rotting wooden frame covered with broken glass and hanging askew. It was part of a beautiful poem—a famous poem— Thanatopsis, written by 17-year old William Cullen Bryant in 1911. It read:

"So live, that when thy summons comes to join
The innumerable caravan, which moves
To that mysterious realm, where each shall take
His chamber in the silent halls of death,
Thou go not, like the quarry-slave at night,
Scourged to his dungeon, but, sustained and soothed
By an unfaltering trust, approach thy grave,
Like one who wraps the drapery of his couch
About him, and lies down to pleasant dreams".

A tiny light hinted on the ceiling of the motel room. Michael strained to greet the light as it twinkled. He stared at the light as it grew larger, brighter and all-encompassing. The light became his focus, his reality. Michael luxuriated in its intangible serene radiance. The brilliant, powerful light enveloped him in Omnipotent Love.

In the morning Michael woke from his disturbing dream—or did he?

Moral of the story: You decide.

Bonus Story: Last Flight Out

Word Count: 571
Reading Time: two minutes 15 seconds

Czeslaw and Irina Czarnina are driving slowly home from the airport with the fuel gauge flashing the empty warning. All the gas stations are dark. The streets are empty.

The Polish couple missed the last flight out—back to Gdansk—when some important, rich guy muscled in on their reservation.

The category five hurricane is riding an apocalyptical wave that will drown them in a 20-foot storm surge. The Czarninas are trapped in a catch-22: no place to go and no way out, no place to hide, no planes, no trains, no buses and no gas.

The Keys are no place to be when Doomsday is playing at the local movie theatre and Mr. Styx is next door and coming your way.

It was curious living in Key West for the last year, watching roosters strut down the streets and observing the libertine lifestyle of naked bicyclers in the Halloween parade. And something told Irina they shouldn't have moved to America, it wasn't for them, but Czeslaw kept insisting they could make a better life for themselves here.

Irina is thinking: a land of hurricanes and storm surges, yes; a land of opportunity, not so much, not today, anyway.

Irina plays with the amber bracelet on her wrist, her signature piece, a small treasure she brought along to remind her of home on the Baltic and the honey-colored amber that abounds there. The bracelet won't do her any good anymore. Possessions mean nothing; survival means everything now.

The two invested every zloty they brought with them into the tiny little bungalow they bought on Pohalski Street. In three hours they'll be manatees and alligators in their living room, maybe an armadillo from the front yard. But the Polish couple won't be living in it. They won't be living.

Czeslaw and Irina can do nothing but wait. The wait is painful. They're not going anywhere, but the storm surge will be going everywhere.

The one-way in, one-way out bridge to the mainland is shut down. There's no one to rescue them because they can't get through. What do you do when you're trapped and you know you're going to die in the worst environmental disaster ever to hit the Keys?

The husband writes his name on his wrist, then writes "Irina Czarnina" on hers so their bodies can be identified when it's all over. Czeslaw pours both of them a shot glass of Krupnik.

The childless couple hold each other tightly, she with her arms around his neck and his encircling her waist. They stay that way for a long time, rocking back and forth and saying their prayers:

Ojcze nasz,

Ktorys jest w niebie swiec

Sie imie Twoje…

The water is up to their waists from the constant rain and the hurricane isn't even here yet. The furniture is floating and their lives are floating away as well.

Suddenly, they hear sounds of life outside in their front yard. They trudge through the water to look out the window. A guy in an airboat is riding on their flooded lawn, waving to Czeslaw and Irina.

"Come! Come!" he says, "Get in! I heard you missed the last flight out."

Czeslaw and Irina Czarnina look at each other, stunned.

"Who is he? How does he know that? Where did he come from? And how did he find us?"

Don't even ask!

Moral of the story: You write the happy ending.

About the author:

Mary B. Good is an award-winning author of five books and enough newspaper people features, columns, and magazine articles with which to wallpaper an entire house.

Yes, Mary B. Good is her real name, and don't ask a lady how old she is, unless you're looking for trouble. This collection could only

Photo credit: Glamour Shots

have been conjured up by a skewed brain that refused to close down at night and an insomniac on the verge of insanity.